HOT SEAL, RUSTY NAIL

A SEALS IN PARADISE NOVEL

TERESA REASOR

SEALS IN PARADISE
HOT SEAL, RUSTY NAIL

Contact Information: teresareasor@msn.com

Cover Art by Elle James & Tracy Stewart
Edited by Faith Freewoman

Teresa J. Reasor
PO Box 124
Corbin, KY 40702

Publishing History: First Edition 2018

ISBN-13: 978-1-940047-22-5
ISBN-10: 1-940047-22-6
Print Edition

TABLE OF CONTENTS

CHAPTER 1

CONNOR EVANS STEPPED into the dimly lit restaurant, whipped off his sunglasses, and paused to let his eyes adjust. The door swung shut behind him, closing out the humid South Carolina summer heat.

He took a seat on one of the leather stools and rested his hands on the bar while he waited to be served. When his phone vibrated against his hip, he jerked it free of his belt case and swiped it with a thumb.

His Dad's terse text language sent one brow climbing. He'd split for a while to put some distance between them. Without his mother there to act as a buffer, they butted heads over everything. Or so it seemed. If the old man had told him he'd be out for the evening, he'd have stayed at the house.

Or maybe not. Everywhere he looked there was something his mother had crocheted, painted or arranged. When he was deployed or training, it kept the loss at a distance. But now, just walking into the house empty of her presence slapped him upside the head and the heart. His grief over her death, as well as an experience during his last deployment, had stirred up other wounds.

The bartender, a tall, lanky guy with an earring and goatee, paused in front of him. "What can I get you?"

"A rusty nail over rocks with a twist of lemon." Connor slipped the phone back in its pouch.

"You got it." The man turned aside and reached for a bottle of blended scotch and one of Drambuie. In record time he was setting the drink in front of Connor and pushing a lemon slice on the edge of the glass for a garnish. "Haven't mixed one of those in a long time."

"I haven't had one in a long time." Six months at least. A beer or two was the strongest thing he'd permitted himself since returning from South America. He reached for his wallet and placed a ten-dollar bill on the counter. The bartender swept it up and handed him back four dollars in change.

Connor sipped the drink, holding the liquor in his mouth, savoring the smoky, honey-citrus flavor of the cocktail. He looked up and caught the gaze of a woman sitting across from him in the dining area. Dark hair and brows, tawny brown eyes with thick lashes, high, flat cheekbones, slender nose, and a lush mouth that gave a man ideas. Gave him ideas.

A woman was something else he hadn't enjoyed in nearly eight months, and right now he wanted one. Wanted her.

Her gaze dropped away and she leaned forward to listen to something the friend on her right was saying.

He stared into his glass, willing the reaction away. He was here to visit family, and to make one of the hardest decisions he'd ever make in his life. He only had a month to decide whether or not to reenlist.

He had no time for a woman. And one-night stands weren't his thing anymore. He wasn't eighteen years old, he was thirty-eight. His twenty years in the Navy were up, and he needed to stay focused and figure out what the hell he was going to do if he wasn't a SEAL anymore.

He looked up again to see the woman standing next to the table, as were her friends. Two of them had to be sisters. Both had thick, curly, dark hair with warm brown skin, possibly Mexican or Cuban ancestry. He saw their Latin heritage in their rounded chins and wide cheekbones. They were both attractive, but the beauty he had his eyes on had paler skin, and her hair was darker.

The three were leaving, making the decision for him. If he'd intended to approach her and introduce himself, he should have done it two minutes ago. Too late now.

As the three women passed him on the way out, he studied her, struggling to find a reason to ignore the urge to rush after her. Why couldn't she be a skinny little thing? Instead she was a real woman, with lush curves. Her olive skin looked soft. She was beautiful. Regret was already riding him before she ever reached the door.

He dragged his eyes away. He did not have time for a woman. A woman on vacation from…who knew where? He had to fly back to California. He had to go back to reenlist or file his separation papers and finish out his time. From there he didn't know where he'd be.

The door closed behind the ladies and he raised his glass to drain the last of the liquor. He debated about whether to order another and decided one was enough.

He'd stop on the way back to his dad's house and pick up the ingredients so he could fix his own.

A SUMMER SHOWER had fallen while they were in the pub, and puddles of water darkened the street. It would be a steam bath by the time they got back to the condo.

"You really should have spoken to that guy, Sloane. If looks could start a brush fire, his would have." Bernie wove the car through the sprawling shopping center parking area to the exit and followed a pickup truck across two lanes of traffic to head west on the William Hilton Parkway. "He looked like he'd been in the desert a month and you're a Popsicle."

From the back seat, Sloane laughed, then bit her lip. She'd never met a man who could make her wet with a glance. She still hadn't. Because he hadn't followed through. She knew one too many guys who couldn't sustain—especially the one she'd been engaged to. The one who'd called her several days in a row recently. She wasn't interested in anything he wanted to say.

But she had to admit she was disappointed when the guy at the bar didn't come over. She didn't often like facial hair, but his dark brown beard lay against his strong jaw neatly trimmed, and his hair was clipped short.

And his molten gaze had ignited an instant sexual charge.

But it wasn't anything her vibrator couldn't satisfy.

She was done with men. They couldn't be depended on. She was going to concentrate on work and move on with her life. In fact, she'd already started the process, because she knew she'd be happier without one than she'd ever been with one.

She didn't need a man to be fulfilled. But she did need something which hovered just out of reach.

Sheryl glanced over her shoulder from the passenger seat. "You have that look on your face again, Sloane."

"What look is that?"

"That frosty, angry look you get when you're pissed."

"I'm not pissed, Sheryl." She opened the notepad on her phone. "I'm just making a few notes about things to take care of before going back to work."

Bernie spoke over her shoulder. "Thoughts about work are not allowed on this trip, Sloane. You promised."

"You can't expect me to go cold turkey after a year of non-stop activity. And if I don't make notes, I'll forget."

"If you got laid, it would take your mind off of work," Bernie commented, shooting her a look through the rearview mirror.

"Bernie, you have a one-track mind."

"Mr. Rusty Nail back there could have been the answer to your dry spell."

"Bernie—" Sheryl threw up a hand to brace herself as a car rushed up beside them and moved to cut in front of them, scraping the front quarter panel of their rental car. The momentum shoved their vehicle to the left.

Their tires screamed as Bernie slammed on the brakes and fought to stay in their own lane while the crazy driver dodged across and into the left lane and out of the way. But the back of a pickup already stopped at the light rose up in front of them, and they hit the tailgate with a bang and the screech of crushing metal and clatter and crunch of broken glass.

A fainter second squeal of brakes filtered through the explosion inside the car as the airbags deployed in a burst of white powder.

Sloane was thrown forward, her seat belt tightening painfully across her chest and shoulder while white powder floated down to coat the seats, and the smell of something burning hovered on the edges of her awareness.

Time seemed to stop for one beat...then another.

"Bernie? Sheryl? Are you all right?" Shaken, Sloane reached for her seat belt and for the handle on the door. It was locked, and for a moment she panicked and shoved against it. She forced herself to stop. *Breathe. You have to breathe.*

"I'm okay," Sheryl said. "Bernie?" She reached for her sister.

Sloane could see in the rearview mirror that Bernie's eyes were closed, and she didn't respond to Sheryl's touch or voice.

Sloane gripped the door lock, pulled it up, then threw the door open, but paused long enough to lean over and pull up on the driver's side lock as well.

She struggled out of the car and rushed around to open Bernie's door.

"Don't move her," a deep male voice commanded.

She turned, and was stunned to see the hot hunk from the restaurant bearing down on her. He was taller than she realized, and his long legs ate up the distance.

"I've dialed 911 and asked for an ambulance." He stepped in front of her and bent to look into the car. "Don't shake her," he cautioned Sheryl. "The airbag might have injured her neck." He ran cautious fingers over her bleeding nose. "I don't think her nose is broken." He placed fingers against Bernie's throat. "Her pulse is strong and even." He focused on Sheryl. "Are you okay?"

"Yes. A little skinned up from the airbag, but I'm okay."

"I'm going to push on the brake." He nodded to Sheryl. "You

slide the car into park and turn the engine off." He knelt on the asphalt and pushed the pedal with his hand while Sheryl did as he instructed.

When the car was finally off. He turned to run his gaze over Sloane.

"I was in the back. I'm fine." Her shoulder ached. She ignored it.

Cars passed slowly, drivers and passengers rubbernecking.

"Is that your truck?" she asked.

"My dad's. I just flew in for a visit and borrowed it."

"I'm so sorry."

He shrugged one shoulder. "Accidents happen."

Bernie moaned, and he braced a knee on the edge of the door. "What's her name?"

"Bernice, Bernie."

"Bernie, you need to remain completely still." He placed a hand against her forehead, pinning her head back against the headrest and keeping her from moving her neck. Blood covered her mouth and chin.

"There's a stack of napkins stuffed in the center compartment of the truck between the seats. Can you get it for me?"

Sloane rushed to fetch them, and went to the other side to hand them to Sheryl. Pale and shaky, worry for her sister evident in her expression, Sheryl cleaned Bernie's face.

The scream of an ambulance, distant and insistent, came closer every moment.

A police car glided up and a cop got out. He moved immediately to place emergency flares at each end of the accident before approaching them. "The ambulance will be here in just a minute." He nodded toward Bernie. "I'll get your information once she's taken care of."

The EMTs were quick and efficient. By the time they stabilized Bernie's neck, she had regained full consciousness and was cursing the man who had caused the accident with creative zeal. The lower half of her face was pink from the nosebleed, and the rest from the stinging slap of the airbag.

A deep chuckle drew Sloane's worried attention away. Now the worst was over, she found herself trembling.

"I recognize that New York accent. I have a friend who sounds just like her. If she's aware enough to be that pissed, she'll be fine." He rested his hand against the small of Sloane's back in a gesture of comfort. His brown eyes, espresso dark, snagged on her face, intent and warm. For the second time in ten minutes, time stopped. Was he experiencing the same thing?

"She probably has a slight concussion, and she'll have some bruising from being hit by the airbag."

"I'm going with her in the ambulance, Sloane," Sheryl announced from across the car. "I've got her purse and mine."

"Good, because you need to be checked out, too," Sloan replied. "I'll deal with the accident report, get another rental car, and then meet you at the hospital as soon as I can."

"Okay." Sheryl approached one of the EMTs, and they helped her up into the ambulance.

"I appreciate you being so calm and helpful through all this." She offered him her hand. "My name's Sloane Bianchi."

He offered her a firm but carefully tempered handshake. "Connor Evans. You kept it together pretty well, too. I hope you paid for the rental insurance."

"Yes, we did."

Two police officers approached them. One spoke to him. "You can move your truck over to the side of the road now."

The other one spoke to her. "I need you to tell me what happened."

WHILE CONNOR ANSWERED the officer's questions, his attention remained on Sloane. He'd missed his first opportunity to talk to her, but karma didn't need to hit him over the head twice to get his attention. The only up side of this accident was it gave him the chance for a do-over.

Before wandering back over to Sloane, the cop returned his

license and military ID, and told him where he could get a copy of the accident report.

While talking to the rental company on the phone, Sloan handed him a piece of paper with proof of insurance on it and all the information he needed to file a claim besides the accident report. She covered the phone. "Is your truck drivable?"

"Yeah. The tailgate took the brunt of it. I can give you a ride to the hospital and they can deliver another car there."

She eyed him. "Why are you being so nice?"

"Because I waited two minutes too long to speak to you back at the restaurant, and I want another shot."

At the quick curve of her lips, a small dimple appeared at the corner of her mouth.

Aw, hell, he was sunk.

"Why did you wait?"

"Because I'm only going to be here a month, and you probably have a life to get back to in a few days or weeks, too. You're too classy for a one-night stand, and I'm too old. So I was debating options, and then you were gone."

Her smile blossomed and his blood rushed to regions south.

"You're right, I am too classy, but you're not too old. And I'd love a ride—to the hospital."

He knew he was grinning like a fool at her double entendre, but couldn't help it.

She finished her conversation with the rental agency, then hung up. "The police have called a wrecker, and the rental company will deliver another car to the hospital. I'll be right back." He watched the graceful sway of her hips as she walked away to discuss something with one of the police officers.

Connor opened the passenger door for her, and was grateful his father was still the disciplined Marine he'd always been. The interior of the truck was as spit polished as his Boondockers.

Sloane approached him, a small handbag clutched in one hand and a single shopping bag in the other. "You lucked out."

He certainly had.

"We did all our shopping yesterday, so there weren't thirty

bags to transfer from the trunk, just this one."

"There aren't any stores where you live?" he asked, taking the shopping bag with one hand and offering his other to help her up into the truck.

She smiled. "Based on our haul yesterday, you wouldn't think so." Her smile died, and she whipped out her phone. "I'm going to call and see how things are going at the hospital."

He placed the bag at her feet, and caught a whiff of her perfume…something with vanilla or coconut…shut the door, and double-timed it around the front of the truck to the driver's door.

The phone conversation was short and positive. "They've X-rayed Bernie's head and neck, and nothing's broken. She does have a slight concussion, and she's going to have bruises but no permanent injuries. And her nose isn't broken. They want to keep her overnight just as a precaution."

"That might be a good idea."

"And Sheryl just has a few scrapes from the airbag and bruises from the seat belt."

"Good. What about you?"

"I'm okay."

"You're rubbing your left shoulder."

"It's just a little tender from the seat belt. More like a burn than a bruise."

He tossed a searching look her way. "Sure you don't need to be checked out, too?"

"Yes, I'm sure. Are you a trained paramedic?"

"I've had a little medical training. In the military you learn a lot of different things."

"You're a Marine?"

"No. My father is. I'm a Master Chief in the Navy."

"Aren't the Marines and the Navy a little at odds with one another? Kind of like rival football teams?"

Connor laughed. "On the battlefield, no. We're all there for the same purpose—to get the job done. Off the battlefield… I like to call it friendly competition."

"Your father lives here?"

TERESA REASOR

"No, he lives in Beaufort, about forty miles away."

"You didn't drive all this way for a drink?"

"No." There was no reason to go into his mother's death and his father's asshole behavior. "I just needed to get away from the house for a while. And driving is relaxing."

"Well, at least until someone hits you."

"That asshole in the green Volvo cut Bernie off, scraped the side of the car, and Bernie overcorrected, then couldn't stop in time."

"Is that what you told the cop?"

"Yeah. Gave him the guy's license plate number, too. It was hit and run."

"All that was going on behind you, and you were still able to memorize a license plate?"

He was still on high alert, having just gotten back from Argentina. But she didn't need to know that either. "I heard the brakes squeal, and the contact between two vehicles. Saw the Volvo swerve into the other lane in my side mirror." And braced for impact.

"You'd be a dream witness at trial."

"You're a lawyer?"

"Yeah, I'm a corporate attorney."

Impressive. "Where'd you go to school?"

"Harvard." Was that a little reluctance he heard?

"I went directly into the Navy from high school. Took some college classes online, but deployments interfere and I haven't finished yet."

"You could try again. You're never too old to learn."

She was right. He'd learned technical things for the SEALs that also had applications in other industries. And if he retired, he could go back to school and do whatever he wanted.

Clearly fishing for a change of subject, she said, "I think this vehicle may be cleaner than my apartment back home."

He chuckled. "My Dad's a little OCD about his ride."

"What's he going to say about it being damaged?"

"Nothing's so damaged it can't be repaired, Sloane. He'll be relieved to know no one was seriously injured. It's just a truck."

A sign for the hospital came up on the left, and he turned off the parkway onto a side road leading directly to the hospital. He parked in the lot as close to the emergency room as possible, shut off the engine, and held the truck keys in his hand, but didn't make a move to exit the vehicle.

"I'd like to see you while you're here, Sloane, if you're interested. I've been out of the country for the past six months in a place as unwelcoming as it gets, bivouacked with a bunch of loud, smelly guys. You get hungry for the sound of a woman's voice, the sweet scent of her perfume and—other things."

She was silent for so long he thought she was looking for a way to say thanks, but no thanks.

"Walk me to the door," she said, soft and breathy.

Her velvety voice tripped him over into a full-fledged arousal. "Sure." He slid carefully out of the truck and went around to open her door and give her a hand down.

As they strolled across the parking lot to the entrance, her fingers curled around his bicep, and he automatically bent his elbow.

She handed him the shopping bag and retrieved her cell from her purse. "What's your cell number?"

He rattled it off, and she typed it into her phone. His phone signaled a text had arrived.

She took the shopping bag from him, rose on tiptoe, and brushed his cheek with a kiss, her breath warm against his skin. "Thanks for the lift, Connor." She turned and stepped on the mat so the automatic door slid open.

"You're welcome." He tugged his phone free and read the message. *Tomorrow night, 7:00, at the restaurant where we almost met.*

He typed *I'll be there* and sent the text.

She paused in the door, phone in hand, to look back at him. "What do you do in the Navy?"

She'd already agreed to go out with him, so he didn't have to worry that she was interested because of what he did. And for some reason he didn't want to have to bullshit her by saying he was a diver. "I'm a SEAL."

She laughed. Which was the last thing he expected.

"I should have known." Flashing him one last smile, she strode into the hospital.

CHAPTER 2

SLOANE PROPPED A pillow behind Bernie and placed a cold drink, her favorite Dr. Pepper, in a coaster on the nightstand, working hard not to wince every time she studied Bernie's injuries. Her poor friend looked like she'd done thirteen rounds in a boxing ring. It was a miracle that nothing was broken.

"Sheryl's fixing you an ice pack and I've got your anti-inflammatory meds right here." She put the bottle on Bernie's nightstand.

"I'm good. You don't have to worry about me, Sloane."

When she first saw Bernie this morning it had scared the shit out of her. Her friend's face was red, tinting toward blue in spots, and her eyes were swollen, the left one almost shut.

So Sloane needed to worry just a little. She didn't know how she'd function if something happened to Bernie. She wasn't just a paralegal and her administrative assistant, she was her best friend and her right hand. "If the tables were turned, you'd be hovering over me."

"As your admin, that's my job. Hovering. And trying to antic-ipate what you might need at any given time."

"And you do it brilliantly. And maybe it's time for me to walk a little while in your shoes and return the favor."

"Actually I'd rather sleep. They kept waking me up every hour on the hour all night. No one can rest in the hospital. You have to go home to get some sleep."

"Okay. Would you like some food before you take a nap?"

"No. I'm not really hungry. I just want to sleep."

"Okay. If you need anything, just call my cell or Sheryl's."

Sheryl brought in the ice pack and Sloane slipped out.

She stood at the sliding glass door to the condo, and was looking past the balcony to the pool below when Sheryl joined her.

"The doctor wouldn't have released her if she wasn't going to be fine," Sheryl said as she stopped beside her.

"I know. We got lucky."

"The ER doctor said Mr. Sexy was right to limit her movements. I didn't realize that something designed to save your life could actually cripple you."

Sheryl looked close to tears, and Sloane gave her a quick one-armed hug. "But she isn't crippled, and won't be."

"No, thank God." Sheryl ran a hand over her eyes and drew a deep breath. "So, how'd it go with your Mr. Light My Pants On Fire With A Look? We were so focused on Bernie last night, I forgot to ask."

It didn't take much effort to bounce her thoughts back to him. "His name is Connor Evans, and he's very nice. He even gave me a ride to the hospital."

"You actually got into the truck with him? I distinctly remembering you saying, 'I'll never trust another man. Not even if he has a halo super glued to his head and a note from God.'"

"Well…" She cocked her head. "Actually, I'm meeting him for dinner tonight."

"OMG!" Sheryl's eyes widened and she clutched her chest, pretending to stagger from the shock. "He must be Superman to have convinced you to have dinner with him."

"Close, but not quite. He's a Master Chief in the Navy." She didn't know why she didn't tell her about his SEAL status. Possibly the remark about him being Superman. She wouldn't date a man just because he was an elite soldier any more than she would because he was the CEO of a multimillion dollar company.

She'd been drawn to Connor's sexy smile and his dark brown eyes. She'd sensed he might be military from the way he stood and moved, and from his calm during the accident. And he'd reeled her in with his forthright honesty while they sat in his truck outside the hospital.

And the look of open hunger he directed at her in the restaurant.

That look triggered an answering ache deep inside her that sprang to life again every time he looked at her last night. She'd never experienced anything like it.

"So where are you going for dinner?"

"I thought we'd meet at Reiley's, where we first saw each other."

"That has a certain symmetry to it. Bernie will be thrilled."

"You don't think she'll mind me going out tonight, right after her accident?"

Sheryl made a scoffing sound. "No. Well that isn't quite strong enough. It's more like *hell, no*. She's been worried about you since the breakup. She thinks you need to get back on the dating horse."

Bernie had harped on it with her, too. But she'd been emotionally numbed when the man she trusted to have and to hold her walked away two weeks before their wedding.

It wasn't his decision to walk away that did it, though. It was his stated reason for rejecting her. He left her feeling damaged, and she didn't know if she'd ever again feel whole.

So what was she doing now? Why was she starting something that couldn't go anywhere?

Maybe because it couldn't go anywhere for Connor, either. He'd be going back to his life after a few weeks, and so would she. She could have a fling without worrying about lasting emotional repercussions.

"I'm just going to enjoy spending time with him. He'll go back to his Navy career when his leave is over, and I'll be going back home to mine. There won't be time for anything special to build between us."

"Why couldn't there be if you both decide you're right for each other? You can work from anywhere, Sloane. You're brilliant, and you're beautiful. And your record with the company is stellar. Any corporation would jump at the chance to hire you."

But not any man. There would always be that one huge hurdle she couldn't overcome.

"You sure you don't mind me slipping off tonight and leaving you and Bernie to fend for yourselves?"

"Of course I don't." Sheryl shook her head. "You've worked like a demon for the past year, and you deserve to take the time to relax and cut loose a little."

"Thanks, Sheryl." Tears rushed in, and she blinked to cover her emotional reaction. "How about some sweet tea? I think my blood sugar is low." Must be why she was feeling so weepy.

She was going to meet a handsome man. A man who could make her weak at the knees with just a glance. A man who triggered a sexual buzz like she'd never experienced before. She needed to focus on that and nothing else, and enjoy her vacation.

"Mind if I change into my bathing suit and lie out by the pool while Bernie's sleeping?" Sheryl asked.

"No, of course not. I thought I'd fix something for lunch while I'm in a domestic mood."

"Sounds good."

Sheryl went in to change into her bathing suit while Sloane brewed the tea on the stove. She added the sugar to the hot liquid, stirred it until it dissolved, then added a few ice cubes to cool it. When Sheryl came out with her towel, sunglasses perched on her head and her cell phone in hand, Sloane handed her a thermal cup of the iced tea.

"Thanks. I checked on Bernie, and she's resting. I'll have my cell with me if you need me."

"Okay."

Sloane spent some time cooking a chicken dish with penne pasta in a creamy parmesan sauce for lunch, and fixed a salad. She'd just opened the oven to take the casserole out when Bernie came out of the bedroom.

"Something smells good."

"It usually is good. It'll have to cool a minute before we eat. Can I get you something to drink?"

"Some of that sweet tea would be good." Bernie sat down at the small kitchen table as though every move hurt, her naturally curly hair standing up in a tangled mess. Plus the swelling along her cheekbones and around her eyes hadn't receded yet.

Sloane filled two glasses with ice and poured the tea over it. She joined Bernie at the table. "How are you feeling?"

"Sore as hell, but it'll pass. I look like hell, but I won't for long."

She never admitted it when she felt like shit. So it had to be bad. Born and raised in New York, she needed everyone to see her as strong as the city she came from.

Sloane played along, "You can tell everyone you got mugged on vacation and kicked their asses. Sheryl and I will back you up."

"I want to tell them I've taken up kickboxing and had a match this week."

"You won big, and took no prisoners."

"Fuckin' A." She shot up a thumb and took a drink of her tea. "I think I need to go home, Sloane."

She said it so bluntly, a beat passed before Sloane could process it and react. She quashed the brief feeling of disappointment. Not because their plans would be canceled, but because she'd miss the opportunity to spend more time with Connor. This was Bernie. She was her best friend. She came first. "Okay. We'll pack up and drive back. It's only two hours."

"No. I don't want you to cut your trip short because of me. Sheryl and I talked about this when she came in to check on me. She'll drive me home in the morning." Bernie covered her hand. "Paul wants me home where he and the kids can look after me, and you need this break. You know you do. Emotionally, physically you're exhausted and so am I. I won't feel like hanging out at the pool or doing much for most of the next week or so. And I refuse to be a drag.

"Sheryl was going to have to drive back on Tuesday anyway

since she only had a couple of vacation days left. Hell, it will take that long for her to do her laundry."

How would she feel about being here alone? What if Connor turned out to be a creep? She didn't believe he would, but...and there were the calls from Reed she'd been ignoring.

Reed didn't know where she was staying. And he only had her cell phone number.

For that matter, Connor only had the same information. If things didn't work out tonight, she could always pack up and go home with Bernie and Sheryl in the morning.

"I'll stay on for a few days at least and just rest."

"I want you to give Mr. Rusty Nail a shot."

Heat rose in Sloane's cheeks, and she stood to get out plates and silverware. "Why are you calling him that?"

"That's what he ordered to drink yesterday. I watched the bartender make it, and I recognized the ingredients from when I tended bar. You might want to lay in some Johnny Walker and Drambuie so when you invite him to dinner you can fix it for him. You'll need a shot glass to measure the liquor, and some lemon, too."

"He doesn't know where I'm staying. That's why I just told him I'd meet him."

Bernie reached out to grip her wrist when Sloane laid the plates out on the table. "You'll eventually want him to know. Look, Sloane, Reed pulled the wool over my eyes too. And I thought I was the best judge of character there is. You can't let one douchebag define every relationship you have from now on. Mr. Rusty Nail—"

"His name is Connor."

"Connor didn't have to stop and help us, help me. He could have just sat in his truck and waited for the cops to show up. Instead, he came back to see if we were okay, helped get the car turned off and in park, and helped you get to the hospital after you talked to the cops."

"He also gave them the license plate number of the car that hit us."

"I hope they catch the bastard. And that doesn't sound like a douchebag to me. A douchebag would have been more worried about his vehicle than us, and pissed off that we damaged it. But then I haven't met him yet. I'd like to thank him and find out if my asshole detector still works."

Sloane laughed. "All right."

Sloane picked up her cell phone from the counter and texted Sheryl to come join them for lunch. Then she texted Connor the address of the condo and an invitation to come over before their date.

CONNOR BRACED A hand against the white tiles in the shower and, leaning into the water, let it stream down between his shoulder blades and rinse away the sweat. Helping his dad put in some landscaping for a client had felt...good, useful, ordinary.

And he needed the activity. Jogging at five-thirty every morning wasn't getting it done. Though the accident hadn't been his fault, he owed the old man since he'd returned home the day before with a caved-in tailgate. Surprisingly, his dad hadn't blamed him. He'd even been cordial while they worked together.

Connor wondered how long it would last.

What had caused this rift between them? He used to call his mom or email every week, whenever he could. Did Facetime with them both on the computer. He'd even tried to continue with his father after her death, but half the time his messages were ignored. He tried calling, and only got the old man half the time, and after nearly two years, here he was, being treated like an unwanted visitor.

Sure, his visits were short, and far less frequent than he'd like. He'd been training, injured some of the time, and wheels up most of the time. SEAL life was hell on family relationships of all kinds. But his dad understood that. He'd been a Marine for thirty years, for God's sake.

Connor couldn't think of a damn thing he'd done that could

have caused this. And eventually he was going to have to take the bull by the horns and face off with his dad to find out what the hell was going on.

His close-cropped hair was still damp from his shower when he exited his bedroom. Dressed in jeans and a blue button-down, short-sleeved shirt for his date, he made his way into the kitchen. He was so used to jungle or desert camouflage BDUs it took awhile for him to adjust to the different fabric against his skin.

He remembered his mom teasing his dad about wearing nothing but khaki or green once he retired from the Marines. The regimented way of life had been hard for the old man to shake, and he still got up at six every day and did PT. Pretty good for a man in his early sixties.

Connor rounded the corner into the kitchen and stopped. His father was sitting at the kitchen table with a woman. A nice-looking woman about ten years his junior. They both rose from their seats. "Connor, this is Dorothy Eads. Dorothy, my son, Connor."

The fine lines around her eyes did nothing to detract from her looks, only added character to a natural attractiveness. A few strands of gray peeked out at the temples of her light brown, sun-streaked hair. She looked fit and lightly tanned.

She stepped forward and offered her hand. Connor took it automatically.

"It's nice to meet you. Your dad has told me so much about you."

Too bad he hadn't said a word to Connor about her. "Do you live in the neighborhood?"

"No. I live in Bluffton. I run one of the galleries there."

He flashed his Dad a questioning look.

"Dorothy and I have been seeing each other for a little while."

His mom had been gone for less than two years. He understood loneliness, but this still gave him a punch to the gut. "How long's a little while?"

Silence hung between them.

"About a year," she said. Her gaze shifted from him to his

father. "You didn't tell him, Toby?"

A flicker of discomfort worked its way across his father's face. "He just got here three days ago."

And he'd been riding Connor's back for two of them. Had it been guilt riding his dad's?

His mom stuck by his dad through transfers and deployments, his less-than-easy retirement transition, then the building of his business. His dad stuck by her through her sickness and death, which somehow seemed to Connor like she'd gotten the short end of the stick.

And he'd been almost as bad. He'd been deployed to the sandbox, and barely made it back in time to see her before she lost her battle with pancreatic cancer.

Between the two of them, who deserved to bear the most guilt?

"What you do is your business, Dad," he managed through a throat that felt like he'd swallowed broken glass. "I have a date. Is it okay if I take Mom's car? The truck is drivable, but it's a little awkward for Sloane to get up in the cab."

"Yeah, sure."

Tobias Evans might be an asshole to his son, but he knew what his priorities needed to be. A lady's comfort always came first.

And Connor had a fifty-minute drive to get his mind straight before he saw Sloane—if he could.

CHAPTER 3

NERVES SENT A tremor through her stomach. It had been well over a year since she'd been on a date. Business dinners, sure, but not a single sit-down with a man she was interested in. They were just going to a bar and grill, but she still wanted to look her best.

She went through the closet and chose a white, short-sleeved blouse and black slacks she bought two days before. The silky fabric would help her stay cool, and she'd wear a camisole under it. And take a sweater in case the air conditioning chilled her. Black, stretchy jeans would create a contrast and make her appear slimmer. A size eight wasn't large, but she was hyperaware of the width of her hips, and the rounded curve of her stomach. Her breasts were what men focused on the moment they met her.

But not Connor. He looked her in the eye. A refreshing change, she hoped.

On her way downstairs, she heard the doorbell and hurried to the door to peek through the security lens. Connor waited on the small covered porch. She opened the door, and the frown knitting his dark brows cleared. He was so damned gorgeous it was hard to not to stare. He smiled as though he read her mind, and she hastened to say, "Come in."

"How's Bernie?" he asked.

"She's bruised, sore, and not feeling too frisky."

"Not unexpected."

"She wants to thank you. She's in the living room." His frown didn't come as a surprise. The man was smart enough to realize he'd been set up.

He cocked his head at her. "I didn't really do anything to be thanked for."

"The sooner you listen to what she has to say, the sooner we can leave." She offered him a coaxing smile.

He grinned. "Am I being vetted?"

"I guess you could say that. Bernie's my legal secretary at work, and my best friend since college. And she convinced she's my watchdog." *But even she was fallible when it came to Reed. A mistake we both made.*

But Connor wasn't Reed, and she was going to give him a chance because all that wild attraction would go to waste if she didn't. "Bernie was out of it for most of the time before, and she wants to meet you before we go out."

"Then I guess I'd better make a good impression."

She slipped her hand in his and tugged him down the hall into the living room.

The bruising on Bernie's face was progressing to a colorful array, and the candy pink top she wore seemed to intensify the effect. Bernie held out her hand to him, and Connor crossed the living room and took it.

"Thank you for helping us. I think we all stayed calmer because you were there."

He patted her hand, took a step back, and sat down on the couch. "I think all three of you ladies are used to holding it together. You'd have done just fine without me."

Sloane hastened to say, "We would have been fine, but it didn't hurt to have a little backup."

"Sloane says you're a Chief Petty Officer in the Navy," Sheryl said.

"Yeah. I went in at eighteen, and I'm finishing up year twenty."

"You seem too young to have spent twenty years in the service."

"I'm creeping up on forty. Not so young, but not rushing over the hill without a fight."

Even though he said it as a joke, Sloane caught the reference and frowned. Twenty years of war, travel, training. She'd done some research since he told her what he did for a living, and learned enough to know there was a lot more to it than she might ever understand.

"Sloane said your father was a Marine," Bernie urged.

"Yeah. Thirty years. He retired six years ago, bought some land, and started his own nursery and landscaping business in Beaufort."

"We saw signs for an Evans' Landscaping coming in," Sloane said.

"Yeah, that's him. We were stationed at Parris Island while he was a drill instructor, and he and Mom really fell for the area and wanted to come back to settle. He has several Marine buddies who've done the same, so they've stayed close."

Bernie jumped on the wording. "You said *we* were stationed."

"Just a slip of the tongue. When you're a member of a military family, it isn't just the person who's serving who's enlisted. It's the whole family. It's a different way of life."

"Are you going to try and stick it out for another ten?" Bernie asked.

"I haven't made up my mind yet. I have a few weeks to decide."

Sloane's head came up. Sounded like he'd reached a crossroads.

The doorbell rang and she bobbed up, anxious to ease them both out of this situation. "That's probably the pizza. I'll get it." She made quick work of paying the delivery person and carrying the box into the dining room.

Collecting her purse and sweater from the hall table, she stepped into the living room. "You two need to eat while the pizza is hot."

Connor, quick on the uptake, flashed her another toe-curling smile and joined her. "It was good seeing you both under better circumstances."

Bernie rose from her seat. "You too, Connor." Sheryl echoed the sentiment.

Sloane was surprised Bernie didn't call out *Don't be late*.

"Think I passed muster?" Connor asked as he closed the condo's door behind them.

"Bernie would have insisted we stay for pizza if you hadn't." They descended the stairs to the parking lot.

"Does she often vet your dates?"

"No. But we're outside our usual territory." And Bernie knew her confidence was shaken. She was a lawyer. She read people for a living. But she hadn't seen the breakup coming. Hadn't seen a lot of the things that steamrolled right over her later.

With a hand against her lower back, he guided her to a Toyota Corolla, hit the key fob, and opened the passenger door. "What territory is that?"

"Charleston." She slipped into the car. It was as clean as the truck the day before, and smelled like the carpets had been shampooed recently.

"Pretty city, nice architecture, and good food, but the traffic sucks."

"Yes, it does."

He continued the conversation as soon as he got behind the wheel. "San Diego is just as bad, and as good, only bigger."

He started the car and turned on the air conditioner. A light whiff of his cologne, something citrus, blended with the chemical smell.

She turned in her seat to face him. "There's something I need to tell you."

His dark eyes focused on her, intent with interest. "What is it?"

"Your father really needs to start his own car detailing business."

His deep chuckle gave her a thrill. Had she ever been this attracted to a man before?

She rested her fingertips on his arm because she found it hard not to touch him. "Thank you for humoring Bernie."

He put the car in gear and backed out of the parking space. "You're her friend. She wants you to be safe."

"She's probably calling your father to check you out right now."

Connor laughed and shook his head. "Before our date is over, I want to know why she's so protective of you."

That was too heavy a subject for a first date. She turned toward him. "It's just the world we live in."

He braked at the stop sign at the corner. His dark eyes scanned her face. "You're in good hands, Sloane."

Her breath caught, and she tried hard to ignore the rush of sensual anticipation shimmying down her body. "I'm not worried, Connor."

THE HOSTESS SEATED Sloane while Connor stood at the highly polished bar and ordered drinks. The same bartender, goatee and earring still in place, moved with quick assurance, setting up a tray of drinks for one of the waitresses.

He approached Connor with a smile. "Hey. Rusty nail, right?"

"Yeah. And the lady will have a California white."

While the mixologist worked his magic, Connor turned to study Sloane as the soft light played over her golden skin and dark hair. The sweep of her lashes, the slant of her brows, gave her face an exotic touch, as did the tawny tone of her eyes. And that lush mouth drove him crazy.

He experienced the same powerful punch of physical need he had the first time he saw her. In fact, it had never stopped. Just thinking of her made him hard.

How the hell were they supposed to scratch that particular itch with her roommates keeping tabs at the condo and his dad's presence at his house?

It seemed sordid to suggest a hotel room. Sloane didn't seem the type to sneak around for a little afternoon delight. But damn, he wanted this woman.

"Here you go," the bartender said.

Connor laid a twenty on the counter, waited for his change, stuffed two bucks in the guy's tip jar, and scooped up the glasses. He set the wine glass in front of her and took the seat to her left.

"When did you start drinking rusty nails?" she asked as she opened her menu.

He grinned. "The guys on my team frequent a bar called McP's Irish Pub. Go there to wind down after particularly tough training days, or to blow off steam. It's run by a retired SEAL. So we were there shooting pool, and one of the guys decided we each needed to choose a signature drink that went along with our nickname. Mine is Hammer. Since I like scotch, I chose a rusty nail, and it stuck."

"Why do they call you Hammer?"

Muscles tensed, he hesitated. She didn't seem squeamish or thin-skinned. If she was, she'd walk away before the night ended. "They say I drop the hammer and take care business."

She lowered the menu and laid a hand over his. "I know you have a dangerous job, and a great responsibility to protect the people you work with, as well as innocent people under fire who can't protect themselves."

She did get it.

The waitress arrived to take their order, breaking the sudden tension.

As soon as she left he asked, "How often do you come to Hilton Head?"

"Twice a year. It's close enough to drive, but far enough away to give me a break from work."

His idea of a break from work was hiking in the mountains or going camping. He couldn't picture Sloane sleeping in a tent or cooking fish over an open fire, but he wondered if she'd be open to giving it a shot.

"How long will you be here, Sloane?"

"Two weeks."

"How about we make those two weeks an adventure?"

The consideration in her expression gave him hope. "What do you have in mind?"

"Have you ever been scuba diving?"

"No."

"I'm an expert, and I can teach you the basics in my dad's pool, then take you out in his boat. What about camping and hiking?"

"I was a Girl Scout, and I did both. I do enjoy hiking, but I haven't been camping since grade school."

"Horseback riding?"

"Never."

The finality bumped up against him, and he decided to try a gentle pushback. "The reason you didn't want to?"

She raised one dark brow. "The long way down if I fell off."

He chuckled. "The key is not to do that."

She studied him. "Why do you want to do all those things with me?"

"So I can be alone with you."

Her tawny eyes looked tiger bright with amusement. "Hoping to get lucky, sailor?"

"That's certainly one consideration."

A slow smile worked across her face, and that small dimple peeked out.

He fought back the temptation to lean over and kiss her and find out what kind of control lay behind that Mona Lisa smile. He took a sip of his drink to ease the need. "There's another reason."

"What's that?"

"I want to lay hands on you, and if I'm instructing you, I'll get to do that."

A bit of color rushed into her cheeks. "Scuba diving seems a challenge, and I'm up for challenges, but it'll be expensive, and I always pay my way. And I like hiking, but not the arduous kind where you're trying to reach a steep summit. I'd rather enjoy the scenery and take some pictures. And I might be persuaded to get on a horse, depending on how the horse and I get along. But I won't camp out. The mosquitoes think my Italian blood is candy, there are chiggers hiding behind every blade of grass, and I have a perfectly good bed in a mosquito- and chigger-free zone, and I intend to use it."

Connor laughed. "I take it you didn't have a very good Girl Scout experience."

She picked up her wine glass and took a sip. "We aren't even going to discuss the poison ivy issue."

He laughed again. "Okay. No camping out. But you're going to miss out on sleeping under the stars." Among other things.

"I'll get one of those machines that projects the constellations on my bedroom ceiling and use my imagination."

"What about fishing?"

"I'm good with that, but you have to clean what I catch."

He shook his head. "Uh-uh. The rule is, you catch it, you clean it."

She moved her shoulders as though shrugging off something uncomfortable. "Okay. I'll concede that. Although you're assuming a lot. We haven't even made it through dinner yet."

"I'm not worried, Sloane."

CHAPTER 4

NIGHT WAS ONLY a breath away as they walked down to the beach from the condo parking lot. The gunmetal gray of the water battled with the rain clouds rolling closer from the distance, and a strong breeze tugged at their clothes when they bent to remove their shoes. She folded up the bottom of her jeans.

"This'll probably hit some time during the night and blow through pretty quickly. It should be clear tomorrow. We could start your scuba lessons then."

"You really are persistent."

"Yeah, I am."

His matter-of-fact tone triggered a chuckle. They'd already laughed a great deal tonight, and it had lightened her spirit. She needed it after her year from hell.

Sloane had never experienced such an instant connection with a man. Not even Reed. After three years together, she'd believed they shared a strong relationship. She was wrong. He wasn't who she thought he was.

In a way this no-strings adventure was easier to deal with. She could just enjoy Connor. And she *was* enjoying him. "What time?" she asked.

"I'll have to get the tanks filled and checked, and I'll see if Dad still has Mom's equipment. If he does, you won't need anything. If not, we'll have to stop at one of the scuba shops and pick up a wet suit and mask. Since you're on vacation, I assume you'll want to sleep in. How's a little after ten?"

Would Bernie and Sheryl be gone by then? She still hadn't told him they were leaving. "That sounds fine."

"We'll start out slow, just do some snorkeling in the pool so you can get used to a mouthpiece, swim a little, and go over the equipment."

The hardest part would be to put on a bathing suit to do all those things. She was no swimsuit model, and she wondered several times during the course of the evening why he was attracted to her. "So your whole family scuba dives?"

"We used to." He looked out to sea, his features still. "My mom passed away two years ago. Pancreatic cancer. The old man and I haven't been diving together since."

It was the first serious note in their conversations.

"I'm sorry."

The waves rushed up on the beach, turning the powdery cream sand to a grayish-tan. The water chilled her toes and splashed her ankles.

"Thanks." He gave her hand a squeeze.

He guided her up on the finer sand when the waves hit a little harder, and moved to block some of the wind with his larger frame.

"Scuba was one of the reasons I enlisted in the Navy instead of the Marines. I already had experience with it since I'd been diving since I was young. Swam like a fish and ran track in high school. And Dad used to take me out to the target range and let me shoot. I knew I wanted to be a SEAL before I enlisted, so I went in under the SEAL challenge program."

"All of that had to help with the training."

"Yeah, it did. Dad helped me get into the best physical shape I could."

"And now?"

"I get up at five every morning and jog. Lift a few weights. Stay healthy even when I'm not training. It's meant a lifetime commitment to staying in shape."

She couldn't say the same. She'd earned her curves with a job that kept her sitting much of the time. "My day is mostly spent doing paperwork, writing motions, studying financial background searches, writing up contracts, and talking on the phone or going to meetings. Or if we're in litigation, going to court. I do walk quite a bit, and do yoga three times a week."

"It fits your lifestyle, doesn't it? That's what's important."

"Yes."

"You didn't tell your friends what I do?" He paused to look down at her.

"No."

"Why not?"

"I'd trust Bernie with my life, but I was worried that Sheryl would go all fangirl and want to spread it around. So I didn't tell either of them."

"Thanks, I appreciate it. I don't normally tell anyone. And I certainly wouldn't want any fangirls."

Too late. "Why did you tell me?" She reached to brush away the long strand of dark hair that blew across her face, but Connor's fingers got there first and tucked it behind her ear. That small, brief touch made her breath hitch.

"You trusted me when you got into my truck. I trusted you when I told you what purpose I fill in the Navy."

He'd trusted her with a secret. But she couldn't trust him with hers. Besides, there wasn't really any need.

She'd be gone in two weeks, and he'd just view her as a temporary distraction while he was on leave.

And she'd view him as…the first man she'd slept with since Reed.

He would be the forth man she'd slept with…ever.

And she was going to sleep with him.

Not tonight, but when the time was right. When she felt comfortable.

God, she already felt comfortable with him. The way his large hand clasped hers, careful but firm. The way he used his body to shield her from the wind. The way he'd smoothed her hair back.

The way his eyes, so dark, looked directly at her when he spoke to her. The way he smelled in the car, when they were close. Like soap, and something citrus, and him. It made her want to bury her nose in the curve of his neck and breathe him in.

They wandered back up the beach, rinsed their feet under one of the spray showers, and slipped their shoes back on. As they took the winding path leading back to the main road and the condo, she both anticipated his kiss and dreaded saying goodnight.

She hadn't felt nervous about a good night kiss since high school, but her breathing stuttered into choppy as they reached the steps. "You can come in for a drink or coffee." They paused outside the door.

He shook his head. "Bernie and her sister will be eager to pump you about how our date went."

"Yeah, they will. It's been awhile." A year.

"It has been for me, too. Deployments and trainings don't leave much time." He eased in close, slipped an arm around her and drew her lightly against him. "Since the first time I saw you, I've wanted this, Sloane."

His lips hovered over hers brushing, tempting, tasting until need tumbled through her. She rose on tiptoe to increase the pressure of their lips, and he tilted his head to accommodate her, his mouth conforming to hers, urging her response with lips and tongue as his hand splayed against the small of her back, drawing her closer.

She gripped his shirt, holding on as the kiss grew hotter, deeper, desire like a ribbon of heat pulsing through her, challenging her heartbeat to match it.

By the time he broke the kiss they were both breathless. He pressed his forehead to hers, his hands moving restlessly up and down her back. "Jesus, Sloane…" His heart drummed against her palms.

Had she ever heard anything as sexy as his deep voice husky with frustrated desire?

She swallowed in an attempt to moisten a throat dry with need while fighting the urge to press closer. "It'll ease off in a minute."

His beard brushed her forehead as he pressed his lips there. "I'm not sure I want it to."

She didn't want it to either. And for the first time in her life she seriously considered having sex on the first date. She'd just met him, but if Bernie and Sheryl weren't sharing the condo with her...

When she realized she was still clutching his shirt, she released it and smoothed the wrinkles, then rested her head against his shoulder, and his arm tightened to hold her. The gesture was so tellingly tender and protective, a knot tightened her throat.

His heartbeat eased to a more normal beat, but the way he released her showed a reluctance that made her smile.

She swallowed and said, "Be careful on the way home."

"I will." He brushed her lips with his once more.

She waited until he'd reached the base of the stairs before saying, "I had a wonderful time, Connor."

The golden glow of the porch light illuminated his features and made his eyes look inky black. "Me, too. I'll call you in the morning."

CONNOR HIT THE key fob to unlock the car as he watched Sloane slip inside the condo. He got into the vehicle. "Jesus—" He'd been with more than his share of women, but he'd never wanted one like this. His heart was still pounding, and he was so hard it was painful. This was crazy. And a little over the top for him.

What if they had all this chemistry and the sex was a bust?

No way. He enjoyed being with her too much. And she was just as into him.

He started the car, backed out, and pulled out into the quiet street.

He'd have to make it clear that things would need to remain casual. A two-week hookup could not lead to anything more. If he decided to stay in the teams, he'd be better off staying single. Keeping a relationship going when you were gone three-quarters of the time was not realistic.

But it wasn't the time apart that caused his and Cynthia's breakup. He veered away from memories still too painful to visit and focused on the to-do list he'd need to take care of in the morning before he called Sloane.

It was nearly eleven when he pulled into the driveway. The two-story, vintage Lowcountry home had a tin roof, dark green shutters, and a dark red door. The dangling lantern lights on the wraparound porch were off, but a single lantern mounted on a pole at the base of the steps shone brightly enough for him to see his father sitting in one of the rockers.

He parked the car in the drive instead of pulling it into the garage and got out.

"How'd the date go?" his father asked as he climbed the steps.

"Good. She's a lawyer from Charleston, with a wicked sense of humor and a quick mind."

"Sounds like you like her."

"Yeah. I do."

"You never had any trouble reeling them in."

He just couldn't keep them. The muscles across his shoulders tightened. Damn the old man for bringing any of this up. "Is that a dig about the divorce?"

"No, Connor, it isn't." Toby leaned forward and rubbed his hands over his face. "Your mother and I never said anything to you about it because we realized the loss would either bring you closer together or tear you apart. We loved you both, and there was nothing we could do to help either of you get through any of it."

Connor raked his fingers over his close-cropped hair. Five years had passed, and he still ached just acknowledging what had happened.

"Even after all this time, Cynthia still sends Christmas cards every year."

"She does to me, too, Dad. We're no longer together, but we still care about each other."

"What about that woman you lived with for a time? Kate, was

it?"

"That was nearly two years ago, Dad. She had to travel for her job, too, and got tired of coming home to an empty house. We called it quits after eighteen months."

But he'd only been home about a third of that time. That final attempt at a long-term relationship had convinced him he needed to remain single.

Unless he decided to leave the teams.

But he loved what he did. Had developed lasting friendships with the guys he worked with. Was addicted to the adrenaline high he experienced when they jumped or went into action or did a million other things that would no longer be part of his life if he separated from the Navy.

And he needed the action, the constant activity, to hold other things at bay. Like the elephant of grief that sat on his chest if he had two minutes to rub together. Between a situation during their last deployment and his mother's death, the old wounds seemed to be seeping again. He tried to stanch them, but nothing was working.

He ripped his thoughts away from brooding. He could use some of the skills he learned during training. He could do more than provide security or blow things up. And he had no interest at all in applying for a position at any of the privately-run security firms that deployed to places as dangerous as the ones he already visited.

He would either be a SEAL or something entirely different.

"You're almost forty. Do you intend to remain alone until you retire?"

"I haven't intended anything, Dad. It's just turned out that way. But I do know I don't want any more children." His words came out sounding raw, which he hadn't intended.

Tobias remained silent a long moment. "I understand your reasons, Connor, but you're denying yourself and anyone you might come to love the opportunity to share all that you have to give."

"I can't, Dad."

What the hell was wrong with his father? It was almost like he'd waited to ambush him with all this. It should have been him doing the prying into this woman he'd taken up with. He shoved to his feet. "I'm going to bed. I'll call Sloane to come over tomorrow, and I'm going to give her some instruction in scuba in the pool. Do you still have Mom's equipment?"

"Yeah, it's in the garage. But the whole rig needs to be checked, and the tank probably needs to be filled."

"I'll do it. I'm just going to do some snorkeling with her to-morrow to get her familiar with using a mouthpiece, and to find out how strong a swimmer she is."

"Good idea."

"About the woman who was here." He eased up on it, be-cause he was still raw about his father finding a replacement for his mother after less than a year. He felt betrayed on her behalf. She was the one he'd call as soon as he got home. The one he did FaceTime with as soon as it became available.

He'd barely gotten to see her and tell her he loved her before she was gone. Had so infrequently been able to visit. But she'd been the only woman in his life he could depend on for uncondi-tional love, and now she was gone. Every time he thought about it it hit him like a two-by-four.

"Dorothy."

His father's voice dragged him back from his thoughts and his grief. "I've been alone for longer than I've had someone waiting for me...for most of my SEAL career. I understand loneliness. And I understand the need for female companionship, sex. But don't expect me to accept her with open arms. I'm not ready for that. All I can do is stay out of your way."

"This might not be as big a deal as you're making it."

He'd never known Tobias Evans to waffle on anything, but he was doing it now. "If it wasn't a big deal, you wouldn't have made a point of introducing me to her." He started into the house, then paused. "How many months was it, Dad? Three? Six? Or did it start before Mom died?"

"No. I was always faithful to your mother, Connor. But after she was gone... And after you were gone... The house was empty, and everywhere I looked was a reminder of what I had, what your mother and I had, and it was... I didn't want to come home anymore."

Just as it had been after Livy died. Then again when Cynthia left. He focused on his dad's face. "You can't screw yourself clear of it, drink yourself clear of it, or work yourself into exhausted oblivion. And you can't replace what you've lost. It just doesn't work."

He went into the house and let the storm door shut behind him.

In his room he stripped down to his boxer briefs and lay atop the spread as grief and anger warred with guilt. He couldn't control how he felt.

An abstract shadow of waving branches played across the ceiling, and he focused on that while he did deep breathing exercises to leach some of the tension out of his body.

By the time Cynthia left, he'd been near his breaking point. He'd thrown himself into his work because it was all he had. He took risks for which his command had cautioned him, and drank more than he'd ever done before, even as a BUD/S trainee. None of it had numbed the pain.

Finally he took every possession, picture, or trinket belonging to or reminding him of his ex-wife and his daughter and put them in storage.

Finally had to turn his emotions off to move forward. But he never truly healed. And his mother's death ripped off the flimsy Band-Aid he put on the wound.

He hoped Sloane would distract him from some of it. He'd laughed more with her tonight than he had in a long time. She somehow eased the angry knot of grief and pain that had settled in his chest, and made the evening a pleasure.

And he could return the favor and give her some experiences she never had and some she'd had, but not with him. Thinking about her was easier than thinking about the situation with his father and the decision that still hung over him.

If only he'd brought her home with him.

CHAPTER 5

WHILE BERNIE AND Sheryl packed to leave, Sloane grated cheese into a bowl, then cracked eggs into another and beat them. When the two emerged from the bedroom and piled suitcases and other bags against the wall just inside the door of the condo, she said, "You need to eat before you go."

"It's only a two-hour drive, Sloane. We can survive for two hours."

"I've already got everything ready, and just need to cook the eggs. Coffee is already fixed, the bacon's already fried, and the toast is in the toaster."

Bernie's bruising was darkening, and she looked like she'd taken a severe beating. "You don't have to feel guilty because we're going home early, Sloane. You footed the bill for the condo and the rental car."

"I feel guilty because you were hurt."

"You weren't the one who hit us and caused us to crash."

"No. But I'm going to miss having you and Sheryl here with me."

"You'll appreciate the privacy when you and your hot sailor start doing the horizontal mambo. I believe he's a keeper."

"He's not interested in being kept. Only in having a good time for the next two weeks."

Bernie studied her face. "Not every relationship is meant to last forever."

"I haven't told him you two are leaving."

She was discriminating in college and only slept with men she cared about. Her college sweetheart, Marcus Simpson. A fling with Robert Allen in law school that turned into a long-term friendship. And Reed. She'd really believed he would be her last lover.

She shook her head. Why was she being weird about this when she'd already made up her mind to sleep with Connor?

The answer slotted into her mind like a missing puzzle piece. She'd never had sex with someone just for the fun of it. And she didn't know if she could do it.

Sheryl bounded down the stairs. "I'll set the table."

"I'll fix the omelets." Sloane turned back to the stove.

Forty-five minutes later she helped them load the car, both sorry to see them go and glad their absence would give her and Connor some privacy.

Bernie hugged her. "I'll be calling to check on you."

"I'll be fine, but I'll want to hear how you're doing. If you need to take extra time off after this break, do it. You'll need to be at your best when we go back."

"I'll be fine too. I'm a little sore is all."

Bernie was lying through her teeth. She'd barely been able to chew her food without pain.

She turned to hug Sheryl and whispered in her ear. "Please take care of her. And if there's any issue, please call me. I'll come straight home."

Sheryl gave her a squeeze. "She's going to be okay. It's just going to take some time."

"I'm sorry you can't stay."

Sheryl grinned. "I'll invite myself again next time."

"You do that."

"Have fun with Mr. Tall, Dark and Dangerously Hot."

"He's going to teach me to scuba dive. I'll learn a new skill and have fun."

"Sounds exciting. Be careful."

"I will."

She watched while Sheryl turned her car onto the main road and waved one last time, until she heard her cell phone ringing from the front walk. She rushed into the dining area and brushed her thumb across the screen to answer.

When she heard Connor's voice, she smiled.

"I've dropped the tanks off to be filled, and decided to see if you'd like me to pick you up and take you to Dad's to use the pool and do some snorkeling."

"If you give me the address, I'll drive over myself and save you a trip. I've got GPS in the rental car."

"Got a pen and paper?"

She found a pad and pen in one of the kitchen drawers. "Okay. Give it to me." She rolled her eyes at the suggestive choice of words.

Connor fed her the address slowly.

"Do I need to bring anything besides a bathing suit and sunscreen?"

"Nope. I have everything else you'll need."

"I'll leave as soon as I clean up the kitchen. I fixed Bernie and Sheryl breakfast before they left for Charleston."

"They left?"

"Yes. Bernie's husband wanted her to come home so he and the children could pamper her. Sheryl already planned to leave on Tuesday, so she's driving her home today."

"You're not nervous about staying at the condo alone?"

"No. I'm used to being alone. And I'm careful."

"Okay. Well, come whenever you're ready. I'm going to help Dad with some things until you get here."

"Okay, see you soon."

After she closed out the call, she stood for a long moment, just staring at the phone. She needed the attention of a handsome, sexy man to soothe her damaged sense of self-worth and her bruised heart.

But her physical reaction to him was so strong, and she really liked him. He was charming and sexy, and what wasn't to like? But what if she started to have strong feelings for him?

Better to have your heart broken because you care for someone than to trick them into thinking you do and destroying them before you walk away.

With that inner argument settled, she went into the kitchen to clean up.

STANDING IN THE shadow of the house, Connor watched the sun play on the crystal clear surface of the water while he waited for Sloane to come out. He narrowed his eyes against the glare and studied the new landscaping he and his father installed along the pebbled concrete boarder behind the diving board. The row of hibiscus in full bloom added a pop of color and camouflaged the chain link fence that acted as a safety barrier around the kidney-shaped pool. Two lounges stretched on the left, their cushion fabric mirroring the freshly-installed plants, while two white tables with solid green umbrellas stood on the right, surrounded by four chairs each.

His mother had picked out every cushion, table, and chair. But his father had maintained the landscaping and the pool. They'd been a team their entire married life. Forty-three years.

One of the French doors opened behind him, and he turned. Her modest black one-piece didn't look modest at all on her lush figure. Her breasts were perfectly shaped and full, her hips the same. Her waist by comparison seemed tiny, a hand's breadth, and her skin, golden from the sun, provided the perfect contrast to her dark hair. He barely controlled the need to reach for her.

Ah, to hell with it. He slipped an arm around her and drew her in close enough that their bare skin touched. "If ever you give up the law, you could model for Victoria's Secret."

When soft color touched her cheeks he was surprised. Even without makeup, her skin was clear and her dark lashes and brows defined. He brushed the backs of his fingers against her cheek.

Her southern accent exaggerated, she said, "You sweet-talker, you." She ran her fingertips over the front of his T-shirt, right over his nipple, triggering a spike of lust. Following through with that would have to come later, he reminded himself.

Still smiling, he said, "You're not nervous about any of this?"

"I don't know how I'll feel once I get the tanks on and am underwater, but the snorkeling doesn't worry me."

"Good. How good a swimmer are you?"

"I can do freestyle and backstroke, and get from one end of the pool to the other. But I don't swim regularly. And I can't dive at all. Too much of a floatation device." She patted her behind. "I kept trying to reach bottom and never could."

Connor grinned, though he was tempted to pat said behind and change her perspective about that. "While we're diving, you'll have a weight belt that will help pull you down, and a buoyancy compensator that will help you float back up. You'll be fine."

He thought of something else. "Do you have any trouble when you fly, compensating for the change in altitude? The change in pressure underwater can sometimes cause issues with your inner ear if you tend to have difficulties."

"No."

"Have you ever been snorkeling before?"

"Nope."

"It'll be good experience to get used to using a mouthpiece and keeping your breathing regular and even."

Entering the water, he demonstrated the way to clear the snorkel and had her practice it several times. Her eyes looked clear and bright through the glass of her diving mask.

He watched her until he was comfortable with her kicking back and forth across the pool in her flippers, which took some time to get used to. When he joined her, he matched his pace with hers.

When she reached the shallow end of the pool, she stood up and pulled the half mask off.

She was a little out of breath, and the beading of her nipples beneath her wet bathing suit proved a nearly irresistible distraction as she said, "You're like a dolphin swimming next to me. It's so effortless for you."

He kept his eyes on her face but, damn, it was tough. "I've

been at it regularly for years, Sloane. As a kid, a teenager, then as a SEAL. You're doing just fine. This isn't a competition or the qualifying round at the Olympics. This is for fun and entertainment. Now let me show you how to sink beneath the water so you can touch bottom."

An hour later, he went inside to fix them each a glass of sweet tea while she stretched out on one of the lounges in the shade, sunglasses covering her eyes. When he returned, he could tell by her complete relaxation that she'd drifted off to sleep. When his eyes wanted to linger on her, he forced himself to move away. He wasn't a stalker.

He placed her glass on the small table beside her in case she awoke, raised the umbrella at one of the tables, and settled there to look over the paperwork he received from the Naval Support Center about separating from the Navy.

He'd be a regular citizen. He'd have insurance through the military, but would be too young to collect retirement. He'd still be able to go on post when he needed to, go to the PX. Utilize the Naval hospitals or VA hospitals. He could possibly use the GI bill for money for school if he decided to finish his degree. And he'd be on retainer for four years after retirement, still receiving pay, in case they needed to call him back into active duty. That would help. But he'd need a job.

He couldn't picture himself in an office. Right now he couldn't picture himself anywhere but on a chopper or in an aircraft racing to someone's defense at hundred forty knots.

Sloane's phone vibrated on the table, and he glanced at the screen. It was Bernie, and he debated whether he should wake Sloane or let it go to voice mail. He reached for it and punched the icon.

"Hello. This is Sloane Bianchi's phone."

After a moment's hesitation Bernie said, "Hello, Connor."

"Hey. How'd the trip go?"

"Just fine. I thought I'd check in with Sloane."

"We've been in the pool for nearly two hours, and she's fallen asleep in one of the lounges. I can have her return your call as soon as she wakes up."

"That would be good. And it's good she's resting. She's been putting in eighty-hour weeks at the firm, and it's been very stressful on top of that for a couple of reasons. If you could get her to relax some while she's there by herself, it'd be great."

"Is she up for partner?"

"No. It's a long story, and she needs to be the one to tell you. Just tell her I made it home and took a nap."

His eyes lingered on Sloane while she slept, her dark lashes like crescents against her cheeks. Her hair lay in heavy waves against her cheek and shoulder. She was flat-out gorgeous.

And Bernie's comments had triggered his curiosity.

Maybe he could coax her into opening up to him.

CHAPTER 6

S LOANE SURFACED FROM sleep, stretched, opened her eyes, and studied the pale blue sky overhead.

The sound of rustling papers drew her attention, and she turned her head to see the light reflected on Connor's hair, giving it a russet sheen. His eyes, so dark, were focused on some papers.

The air felt heavy and hot, and was scented with flowers and chlorine. She rolled off the lounge, reached for her wrap, and tied it around her waist. Walking over to the pool, she dipped the corner of the cover-up in the pool and gave her face and the back of her neck a cooling wipe.

He looked up as she approached. She slid a hand along his shoulders and felt the firm muscle beneath his T-shirt. He was quick to hold on to her hand and tilted his head back to look up at her.

"I'm sorry. I fell asleep."

"No, worries. Naps are part of vacation. Two hours in the pool earned you a nap. And from what Bernie said about you working eighty-hour weeks, you probably need all the rest you can get."

She frowned. "When did she say that?"

"She called a half hour ago. I told her I'd tell you to call her back ASAP, and she asked me to tell you she made it home and took a nap." He slipped an arm around her waist to hold her there.

"What are you working on?" she asked.

"This is the paperwork I need to fill out if I decide to separate from the Navy."

"I'm good with paperwork. My job is mostly paperwork...and being an immovable barrier when someone is trying get around us."

"Immovable?" His brows went up.

"Yeah, when I have to be."

"Do you like what you do?"

"Most of the time. These last twelve months have been a little difficult because one of the airlines brought suit against one of our companies and I handled the case."

"Which you won."

"Yes."

"What would you do if you had to change careers in four months?"

She thought about it for a moment while smoothing his hair back from his forehead, and was rewarded with one of those looks that made her legs weak and lit a tingling heat in intimate places.

She dragged her thoughts back to his question. "I'd become a dog-walker."

"Why would you want to be a dog-walker?"

"I'd get to spend the whole day in the park wearing shorts or jeans and playing with creatures who'd show me unconditional love. I wouldn't have to prove myself to them, because they'd accept me just as I am." It took some effort to disguise her bitter feelings.

"Care to expand on that?"

"Most people are two different people. One at home and the other at work. You aren't the same man with me that you are with your teammates."

"No, I'm not. But I'm not dating any of them, either. They don't have what I'm looking for, and it's not just the beards."

She laughed. Though he had to deal with much more danger-ous situations, he was insulated from the real world here at home.

He probably didn't realize what the work environment was like for the average woman, especially ones who were bumping up against the glass ceiling. "This work thing is just the way of the world."

"Did something happen at work that preceded your need to be a hard case?"

She sat in the chair on his right. "Why do you ask?"

"The eighty hours a week thing."

She remained silent for a moment. If she avoided telling him and then told him later, he'd think she was hedging. It was time she put it behind her.

"A year ago, I was engaged to a fellow attorney. His name is Reed Alexander." She moistened her bottom lip, though her mouth and throat seemed to have dried up, and she wished for the glass of watery iced tea she left next to her chair. "Two weeks before the wedding, our relationship imploded."

His face settled into solemn lines. "Son of a bitch."

"It gets even worse."

His brows rose.

"Reed decided I should move on to another firm, even though I was hired a year before he was. He is a golfing buddy of the boss's son, and he and Marshal, the boss's son, encouraged Clay, my boss, to make things difficult for me to drive me out. So I filed a lawsuit for hostile working conditions and sexual discrimination."

"That couldn't have been easy."

"No, it wasn't. In fact, it was the hardest thing I've ever done. But I had the proof that I was there longer, had a history of more billable hours, and brought in more business than Reed did, and I presented as evidence the sexist emails sent to me by one of the heads of the company."

"And?"

"The court agreed with me. The firm terminated Reed. But now the partners are putting more and more pressure on me to leave. I'm looking for another job, but until I find the right fit for Bernie and me—because I refuse to leave her behind—I'm not letting them drive me out. I'll leave such a work product history that they'll wish I'd never left. I'm documenting everything, and getting letters of recommendation from all the clients I work for so they can't screw me when I do leave."

"Sounds like you have a handle on things."

"Not really." She brushed a hand over her hair and tucked the long strands on either side of her face behind her ears. "I'm in survival mode all the time. Checking and double-checking my work to make certain I haven't made a mistake they can use to fire me.

"And lately I've been making extra copies of my paperwork, just in case someone tries to mess with any of it."

She rested her elbows on the table and linked her fingers. "I know how it sounds. Like I'm a crazy, paranoid bitch. But it's true. Bernie watches my back. I can't leave her behind, because they'd demote her or fire her outright for being loyal to me."

"Could you start your own firm?"

"With the weight of a big firm against me, I'd never make it. They'll put out the word that I'm a troublemaker, not a team player, or some other kind of bullshit. In order to have some insulation against that, I'll have to move on to a firm comparable to them, or move to a different city."

"Damn." He leaned back in his chair. "What happened to the asshole who started the whole thing? This Reed guy?"

"They asked him to leave to avoid the adverse publicity, and I dropped the suit. But it came out after he left that he'd been screwing at least one secretary and one of the interns while we were engaged."

Going into her doctor to be tested for STDs was as humiliating as everything else he dished out. One more betrayal on top of everything else.

"He, of course, got a glowing recommendation from the boss and landed on his feet with a big firm."

"I'm sorry, Sloane."

She glanced away. "Thanks, but I'm over it. It's been more than a year now. He wasn't the man I thought he was. But I keep wondering why he asked me to marry him to begin with." Had he been that desperate for a place to live? He'd taken advantage of her for that too, which was just as humiliating as the rest.

He reached for her hand. "You're a beautiful woman. Smart, funny. Strong. Isn't that reason enough?"

"Probably more like he thought that by stirring all this up he'd be able to step into my job and take my accounts once I was gone."

"Shit! That's cold."

His masculine face, even crimped in a fierce frown, seemed irresistible. She covered his hand with her own and gave it a squeeze. "You are so good for my ego. I'm really not a psycho bitch."

He leaned forward, a quick smile quirking his mouth. "You don't come across as a psycho bitch."

She didn't want to be an object of pity either. "Now you've heard all about my work issues, we need to concentrate on what it is you want to do once you're out of the Navy. You've got valuable skills and training to offer."

"I don't want to go into security or work for one of the private corporations that ship out to support military units. I might as well stay in if I do that."

"You could be a police officer, a paramedic, or a fireman. You'd probably skate through the training and the physical. And it would give you that buzz you'll miss when you're no longer going into action."

His eyes cut to her and he raised a brow. "Buzz huh?"

"Not my choice of words. I've had several clients who are retired military who now work for businesses I represent or have started their own. I help them get all their paperwork in order. No SEALs, but others. You just have to pour all that energy you used in other ways into what you're building and develop a passion for it."

"I like to be active and outside. I'm good with my hands."

"Massage therapist?" she asked with a teasing smile.

"I'll share my technique with you later," he grinned. "I meant building things and working on engines, boat engines, car engines other engines."

"You could start your own boat business. Working on them and selling them."

He lifted his hand, palm down, and rocked it back and forth. "It would be seasonal, feast or famine."

"Not in California."

"I'm not sure I want to stay on the West Coast. To be there and not be in touch with my guys, not be a part of what we do…" He shook his head. "Dad is getting older. I'd like to settle nearby. He's the only close family I have."

"He'll probably love having you close."

His silence at the comment had her studying him.

"There's been some tension between us. He has a girlfriend. Has had for over a year. I just found out when I got here."

He told her his mother had died two years ago. How would she feel if her father took up with another woman less than a year later? She couldn't go there. Her mom and pop were a unit. They did everything together. "I'm sorry you're having to deal with that."

"I'm a grown man, I haven't lived at home in years, but it just feels—wrong."

"I'd feel the same way in your shoes."

Time to change the subject. "You haven't ruled out going back to school and finishing your degree?"

"No. I've already been working toward a degree in business administration. A little tame compared to what I do for a living, but I thought it might come in handy."

"It probably will. And give you a good background for running your own business. But you're never too old to go back and do something else. I graduated with a guy in his fifties who had gone back to school to become a lawyer."

He narrowed his eyes in thought. "Being in an office day after day wouldn't be my dream job."

"Forest ranger?"

"I'd probably like that. But from what I've heard about all the cuts to state and federal parks, the pay isn't great."

"You could go back to school to be a doctor."

"What kind of doctor?" he asked, a smile playing across his face.

She couldn't resist teasing him. "A proctologist?"

He laughed. "I've already dealt with enough angry assholes. I don't want to have to do it the rest of my working career."

Her laughter blended with his.

They batted a few more serious ideas back and forth. "Your tea has gone to water. Let's go in and I'll get us both some fresh."

She leaned against the kitchen cabinets while he freshened their iced tea.

"It's hard for me to share things. We have to keep so much about what we do to ourselves. I'm used to just keeping things on the surface, and not sharing anything at all." He set the glass on the counter. "My teammates know I'm thinking about leaving, but I haven't even told them... I have an idea for a drone design, and I've already partially drawn it in AutoCAD."

Wow. "That's wonderful! You could do a degree in mechanical engineering. It would just be four years of study, and you wouldn't have to go for your master's or doctorate unless you wanted to.

"The aeronautic field is wide open. Any kind of new design is of interest to the industry. But if you offer it to any of the companies while you're still in the Navy, Uncle Sam can and probably will claim it's work product. So I'd hold off on approaching anyone with that idea at least until you've filed the paperwork to retire."

"I have two more classes to finish the business degree. I could do that first while I'm rotating out of the teams."

"Finishing a degree will give you a leg up to being accepted into a program. Your military experience will help as well. You have to use complex math to do things in your job, don't you?"

"Yeah. Sometimes. Mostly I've taught myself while learning about fuel injection and airflow resistance."

The way his eyes cut away from hers made it clear he was being careful not to mention exactly how he used the math. "You're on your way. And it can't be any more difficult than being a SEAL."

"No, it couldn't be." He set her glass down on the counter next to her, and then hemmed her in with a braced hand on either side. He brushed his lips against her cheek. "Not as hard as it's been for me to keep my distance all afternoon, either," he murmured against her ear, his breath warm.

A shiver skittered down her spine when he nibbled at her lobe. Then he ran his fingers beneath the thin strap running over her shoulder. "This clings in all the right places."

God, she wanted him. She wanted to kiss him and find out if the curl-your-toes kiss last night was an aberration or the real deal. She gripped his T-shirt with one hand, sliding the other up his arm to curl around the back of his neck.

Her heart beat heavy and fast as he nibbled his way down to her shoulder and let his hands wander to her waist. God, she wanted him to touch her, cup her breasts and….more. She leaned back to look up at him. His eyes looked black, the pupils swallowing his dark brown irises. He moved in close until their bodies molded tight. She caught her breath as his erection pushed against her belly.

"I've been thinking all day about the kiss last night. Think it was a one-off, or will every one be the same?"

She swallowed to get her voice under control. "We could give it a try and find out."

He claimed her lips as though he was starved for her. He tasted of the sweet tea and him. Their tongues delved and dueled. He dragged her bathing suit strap down her arm, baring her breast, and cupped it. She leaned into his touch. Her nipple beaded and he toyed with it, rolling it between his fingertips. She shoved her hands beneath his shirt to run her nails lightly down his belly to the top of his trunks. He moaned against her lips.

At the squeak of the front door and the sound of footsteps, he raised his head, swore under his breath, and took a step back.

CHAPTER 7

THE BREAST HE'D uncovered was full and round, with a carmel-colored nipple. He wondered if it would taste as sweet. He pulled the thin cup of her suit up to cover it, settled her strap over her shoulder, then reached for her iced tea and handed it to her.

Her cheeks were a little flushed beneath the golden tone of her skin, as though she'd just come in out of the sun.

His father paused in the doorway. "Hey. How did the snorkeling go today?"

"Good. Sloane's a natural. We're going to try the tanks tomorrow." He ran a hand down her back, the cold turkey withdrawal from her hard to take. "Sloane, this is my father, Toby. Dad, this is Sloane Bianchi."

Toby stepped forward to offer her his hand. "It's nice to meet you, Sloane."

Her narrow hand looked fragile enveloped in his dad's larger one. "You, too."

"I'm going to take a shower and change clothes. Then we'll throw some steaks on the grill. I've had them marinating since early this morning. You'll stay for dinner, won't you?"

"Sure. Thank you for inviting me."

"You're welcome. Why don't you warm up the grill, Connor?"

"Will do."

When Toby disappeared down the hall, Sloane's attention

swung to Connor.

His lips twitched. "I feel like I'm in high school again, and I'm sneaking around to make out with my girl."

The color on her cheeks deepened, and she buried her nose in her glass for a moment as she took a sip, then set the glass aside. "Thank you for…"

He stepped close again and cupped her chin to raise her face to him. He kissed her softly. "You're safe with me, Sloane. Whatever this is we have between us, it's ours." He kissed her again, then dropped his hands. "If you want to take a shower and change, you can use my bathroom while I go light the grill. It's down the hall, second door on the right."

"I'm going to do that." She paused by the door to look over her shoulder at him and offered him a smile both vulnerable and sweet.

Need coiled tight inside him. There wasn't a doubt in his mind that if his father hadn't shown up, they'd be making love right now. He'd never experienced anything close to this intensity of attraction.

CONNOR COULD GRILL. The steaks were tender and done to a turn with just a little pink in the middle. The salad with freshly made dressing, delicious. The zucchini was cooked perfectly, still firm and succulent. The twice-baked potatoes were smothered in sour cream, cheese, and bacon.

Sloane felt the tension between the two men the moment they sat down. But they both made an effort to entertain her. After dinner they moved to the patio out by the pool, and Toby offered her a cocktail, but she declined. She had to drive back to the condo.

Though Connor was taller, Toby Evans had a similarly muscular build. Their skin tones were close, but Toby's hazel eyes seemed less intense than his son's dark brown ones. His hair, liberally sprinkled with gray at the temples, waved back from his forehead.

Connor would look just like him in another twenty years or so. The way they stood and their mannerisms were similar, but Connor's voice was like the rusty nail cocktail he was sipping, deep, smoky, and warm.

"Beaufort's downtown area needs some work. We're getting more tourism traffic than we used to," Toby said as he sipped his Scotch on the rocks.

"Everywhere seems to be," Sloane agreed. "The traffic in Charleston is terrible. If I could order my groceries and have them delivered, I'd never leave the house."

"What's a little traffic to the woman who accepted a two-week-long challenge?" Connor scoffed.

"What kind of challenge?" Toby asked.

The sweet fragrance of the Carolina jasmine climbing the fence reached her, and she breathed it in. "Connor has challenged me to spend this week and next doing things I've never tried before. Thus the snorkeling lessons and the scuba instruction tomorrow."

"What comes after that?"

"Horseback riding," Connor answered.

"After that?"

Sloane jumped in. If she survived the scuba thing and the horseback ride, she'd need a break. "I've never been to hear a jazz band."

Connor's brows rose. "I haven't either. We'll have to hit the Jazz Corner. I heard they have guest musicians performing all summer."

"You'll have to call and make reservations a week ahead. The place fills up pretty quickly," Toby said, and when Connor turned to look at him he added, "Your mother and I used to go."

Connor took a sip of his cocktail. "I didn't know she was a jazz fan."

"She liked all kinds of music. I took her because it pleased her, and I got points for being a good husband." Toby winked at Sloane, and she smiled.

"I was gone so much when Connor was growing up, I felt like I needed to go the distance to make up for all the time we missed together." He fell silent for a moment. "I've been to some wonderful performances at various venues, and some not so wonderful ones. Even went to a few plays and a ballet or two. We could always depend on the Jazz Corner for a quality show. They're usually on Tuesday night."

Sloane looked to Connor. "What do you think?"

He raised his glass to her. "I'll call tomorrow and make reservations for next Tuesday."

She flashed him a smile.

"Connor says you're a lawyer."

"Yes. I work mostly for corporations and a few smaller businesses for Hadley, Childers, and Johnson."

"They're pretty big stuff in Charleston. I see their advertisements all the time."

"Yeah, they are."

Toby leaned forward in his seat. "You have to have a passion for your work to enjoy it. I guess the law for you is the same as me running my nursery."

"Sometimes it is. I help people to establish their companies and help them expand or merge with others. Mostly I create contracts for their employees and generally all the paperwork that goes into starting and keeping a company going."

"Sounds like a lot of responsibility."

"It is. Some are family-run businesses with a small number of workers. Others are large corporations with hundreds of employees, depending on their goals and success."

"I understand the pressure. I have twelve employees including me, and I sign their paychecks every week. You become an ecosystem all your own."

"Yes, you do."

"So you keep everyone working," Connor said.

"Actually, the people who run the businesses do," she replied. "I just try to keep everything legal so they can continue to do it."

The conversation moved to something more general, and after another half hour she rose to leave.

"You sure you'll be okay alone?" Connor asked as she met him at the foyer carrying the tote with her bathing suit, cover-up, sunscreen, and a few towels.

His hand caught hers as they wandered down the steps to her car. "You're welcome to stay here with us."

"I appreciate the offer, but we both know what a temptation that would be. I'll be fine at the condo."

She tossed the tote behind the driver's seat and turned to face him. "Dinner was delicious. You've got some killer grilling skills."

He shrugged one muscular shoulder. "Women cook, men grill." When he offered her a teasing grin, she shook her head.

"You could say you're nervous about staying alone and I could join you," he offered.

She studied the width of his chest because she was afraid he'd read how much she wanted to do just that. "Think your father would buy into that?"

"Not a chance." He leaned back against the car and drew her between his feet, urging her to lean into him with a hand splayed against the small of her back.

"I wouldn't want him to think I'm a loose woman." She swallowed against the ragged beat of her heart and rested her head against his chest. "I'm tempted more than you can imagine."

"I'm counting on it."

She smiled and leaned back to look up at him. "Do I need to bring anything tomorrow?"

"Just you." He tucked her hair behind her ear. "Thank you for being a sounding board."

"You have a lot to think about." And so did she. She cupped his face in her hands and got up on tiptoe to touch her lips to his. He slanted his mouth across hers with a hot enthusiasm that left her wet with need and her legs weak.

"You are so good at that," she murmured when he finally raised his head.

"That ain't all."

She laughed, then shook her head as she dragged herself away from his arms to get into the car. She rolled down the window. "And you're so humble, too."

CHAPTER 8

CONNOR WATCHED AS Sloane rubbed repellent on her legs, concentrating on her ankles and the backs of her knees. Her long tail of dark hair, which was hanging through the slot at the back of a bright pink baseball cap, draped over one shoulder as she straightened. She gave her arms a cursory swipe as well, then handed the bottle to him.

After wiping her hands clean with a baby wipe, she tucked it in one of the pockets of the foot-long backpack she'd brought along. He decided she made even the casual look of red shorts with a belt and a pullover scooped-neck top somehow seem professional.

"We're just going on a short hike, Sloane."

She popped sunglasses on her face and looked over the rims. "You have obviously never been on the biting end of a chigger."

He laughed. He could say he'd been on the biting end of chiggers, sand fleas, flies, mosquitoes, scorpions, spiders, ticks, leeches, the attempts of a snake or two, and one persistent shark that had gotten way too close for comfort, but he wouldn't steal her thunder for the world.

To please her, he spread a little of the repellent around his ankles and calves.

Settling her small, lightweight backpack over her shoulders, she smiled at him while he tucked the bottle of repellent inside a pocket and folded down the Velcro flap for her. How much stuff did she carry in that thing? It couldn't have room for much.

Her skin had already begun to tan, a dusky, warm color despite the sunblock she slathered on.

He was glad to be out in the fresh air and sunshine with her. The temptation to rush her into bed was just too strong, thus the change of plan from sticking around the pool, as they'd been doing the last two days, to a short hike in the local forest preserve.

Under the shade of the trees the sun was blocked enough to keep the walk from being too hot. Their steps clumped hollowly on the wooden boardwalk that meandered through the forest.

Sloane paused, her attention directed at the moss-hung trees overhead. "You could go into the landscaping business with your father. You seem to know a lot about plants."

"My mom was into plants way before Dad went into business. And as for a partnership between us—My dad is a good guy. But we have a tendency to rub each other the wrong way. I suppose because we're too much alike. My mom was always the buffer between us, and now she's gone…" He shrugged. "I'm proud of what he's accomplished, but I want to build something on my own."

"I understand. My dad's a lawyer, and he offered to take me into his firm after I passed the bar. I love him dearly, but I wanted to earn a partnership, not be brought into one because we're family."

"I get that."

"You could apply to be a civilian consultant for the military after you get your engineering degree."

He'd thought about that. "Another avenue to explore in the future."

They came out from beneath the canopy of trees into a section of boardwalk that crossed an old rice field. He grasped her arm and pointed at an egret strutting through the marshy water on pencil-thin black legs. Egrets looked both gawky and graceful on land and in the air. As though he hoped to prove that observation, the bird suddenly spread his wings and took flight, dragging his long legs behind him.

Connor couldn't read her eyes behind her glasses, but he admired the smooth skin of her cheek and jaw, the lushness of her mouth.

"He's gorgeous, isn't he?"

So was she. He nodded. "I've filled out the separation paperwork. I just have to put a stamp on the envelope and mail it."

"It would be natural if you're having trouble taking that last step. It has been twenty years. Being in the military seems to be as much a way of life as a job."

"Yeah, it is. I've already been updating things...my will, my medical files and that kind of thing. Got a copy of my service record. I'll be in reserve for four years after I transition out."

"Does that mean you'll be limited to the areas where you can live?"

"It means that I'll be held in reserve in case of war and they need to call me back to active duty. They spent nearly a million dollars training me, so if they need me, I'll go."

"Once a SEAL, always a SEAL," she mused.

"Same as in any other branch of the service."

She waved away a persistent fly. "If you could use some of your SEAL training on your resume, it would be good."

"Maybe a few things." Although if he put everything down it might make him sound more like a terrorist than a viable employee.

"You could do demolition for a construction companies."

"That's actually plausible, but I'd rather build than destroy."

She shot him a mischievous smile. "You could open a kissing booth and make a fortune."

He laughed. "I'll keep that in mind, just in case." He caught her hand. "I'm a little picky about the women I kiss, though."

"I'm glad to hear that."

Seeing sinuous movement just ahead, he pulled her to a stop and caught her parted lips with his own, distracting her from the snake crawling across the path. After a momentary pause, the warmth of her response had a quick rush of blood going south and his jean shorts felt tight.

A group came up behind them, and he broke the kiss and smiled at her. The snake was gone. He stepped aside for the family to go on ahead of them.

She raised her hand to his cheek. "Thank you for trying to distract me from the snake."

He shrugged. *Busted!* "You're welcome."

"I'm not really afraid of them. Not even the human kind. Or rats. I've dealt with a few of them, too. The worst are the rich ones. I don't like spiders, though. So if you see a web ahead you have my permission to swat it away."

"And this is the woman who worries about chiggers?"

"I don't like to itch."

He grinned. "Depends on what's causing the itch and how it needs to be scratched." They'd been dancing around that for the past two days. But he wasn't going to rush her. She'd let him know when she was ready.

She gave a bark of laughter. "I can't believe you just said that."

He scanned her lovely face. Her sense of humor, the sound of her laughter, were just as much an aphrodisiac as remembering the soft weight of her breast in his hand. "I have a powerful itch for you, Sloane, and I thought a day away from the house might be a smart idea."

Her cheeks pinkened. She looped her arm through his and leaned against him while they walked. "I've always been a little wary of jumping into things too fast. It took eight weeks before I gave into temptation the last time." She rested her cheek against his arm.

And it hadn't worked out very well for her. But he understood her need to get to know him better. He tried to put their limited time out of his mind. "The best things are the ones you have to wait for. What do you say we get some ice cream when we're through here?"

"I'd love that." Her cell phone rang, and she pulled it out of her back shorts pocket and glanced at the number. Her jaw tightened as she declined the call and tucked the phone back into her pocket.

"Trouble?"

She hesitated. "My ex has been calling me."

"You haven't spoken to him?"

"I'm not interested in anything he has to say."

"You could block his number."

"That's a good idea. Do you know how to do it?"

"Sure."

She took out her phone and handed it to him. "Watch me do it so you'll know how." She leaned lightly against his arm while she watched him. Her ex's name was no longer in her contacts, though his calls were in missed calls. He went into settings and blocked the number.

"How long's he been calling?" He handed back the phone, and she tucked it into her back pocket.

"Two weeks."

"How often?"

"Nearly every day." She looked up at him. "The only reason he'd be calling is if he wants something. And I'm not interested in listening to it or giving it to him. Let him waste someone else's time."

If she hadn't answered the phone in two weeks, she really meant it. "You're not curious?"

"No. After looking back over things that happened over the course of our relationship, I decided not to waste another second of my life on him. I'm only wondering why it took me three years to realize I was being made a fool of."

"When you love someone, you don't expect to have to analyze everything they do or say, looking for whatever they're hiding. You want to trust and believe in them." Jesus. Who was he to spout things like that?

But he'd never deceived Cynthia. He hadn't shared enough of himself after everything to deceive her. He'd been too busy running from the pain or trying to dull it any way he could. But he'd never been unfaithful. He hadn't been interested in sex enough to even think about going that route.

"The man I loved never existed, Connor. He was a figment of my imagination. Nothing I thought I knew about the person he pretended to be was true. I was living with a con man and didn't know it."

"If he played you, he must have played other people, too. Your boss, his son. Guys like that don't change. They're all about using the game to get ahead. They thrive on it."

"Sounds like you might have had some experience with people like that."

"Only from a distance. Bad people usually have compartmented lives. They can be the loving father and husband on one hand, and the heartless killer on the other. Nothing's ever black and white with them, but somewhere in between." Like the many drug cartel leaders and members they'd dealt with. Like the terrorists they'd taken out. Some had wives and mistresses, children with each, and killed people in cold blood without a thought.

Like the last asshole they'd been after.

Causing their loved ones' deaths because of who and what they were.

The dreams tormenting him recently seemed to be bringing his own losses to the forefront. But knowing that and being able to control it were two different things.

Sloane's voice dragged him away from those thoughts. "How can they have a conscience?"

"Most of them don't, Sloane. Otherwise they wouldn't do what they do."

They walked in silence for a few moments until they reached the end of the boardwalk and came upon an open spot beneath the trees.

"He could show up on your doorstep. If he does, I'm available." Pounding on the asshole for her might help him deal with some of his own pain.

"Thank you. I appreciate it. But he doesn't know where I am. The only ones who do are my parents, Bernie, and Sheryl. I'm not worried about him."

"Good."

She paused to remove the backpack and opened the top to remove two bottles of water, handing him one and opening the other.

He took a drink. "What else do you have in there besides baby wipes, repellent, and water?"

"A small first aid kit, some power bars, and my ID."

He shook his head. "You've shown me up. All I brought were my car keys, a Swiss army knife, some gum, and my wallet."

"I'm obsessive." She tucked her bottled water into the mesh at the front of the pack.

Cynthia packed things just like that every time they left the house with Livy. Was that kind of preparation instinctive for women?

"You've heard enough about my romantic disappointments. What about you? Any romantic woes you want to get off your chest?"

God, he hated this part. Why couldn't she just act like he'd dropped out of the sky the moment they met? He wasn't ready to own up to his failures. "My last relationship lasted eighteen months, but we were only together about six of that since I was deployed and training a lot of the time. She traveled a lot for her job, and we just couldn't make it work."

"I'm sorry, Connor."

"The life is hard on relationships." And now his mom was gone, the only one he had waiting for him at home was his dad.

He looked up to find Sloane watching him. They only had two weeks. What was he doing, standing out here in the heat with the bugs and a bunch of tourists, when they could be alone together getting to know one another in other ways. "The most interesting part of the preserve is the shell circle here. It's just up ahead. After we've seen it, how about we go back and get that ice cream?"

"I'll be ready for something cold by then."

HE WAS RESTLESS, edgy. Had been since he called to change their plans, then came to pick her up. What had brought it on? And how could she get him to share it with her?

When they pulled into the parking lot across from Munchies—a local deli that served soups, sandwiches and ice cream—he seemed to have settled some.

"We could eat lunch here then go up to Bluffton and check out the art galleries and gift shops if you like."

He released his seat belt. She laid a hand on his arm. "Why don't you talk to me about what's bothering you, Connor?"

"How do you know something's bothering me?"

"You're like a rooster on a hot rock."

He raised a brow.

"I couldn't very well say a hen. You know what I mean. What's got you on edge?"

He rested his fingertips on the steering wheel and ran them around it. Though the silence stretched between them, she waited.

"Sometimes I have dreams about things that happened during deployment."

"After numerous deployments, I'd be shocked if you didn't."

"Some of it is pretty bad."

She released her seat belt so she could turn in her seat.

"What do you do to relieve it?"

"Sometimes I run. I did my five miles earlier. I just have to work through it, Sloane. That's all any of us can do." His dark eyes settled on her face. "I'm okay."

"You know if ever you need to talk about anything, I'll hold it in confidence."

He nodded. "I wish I could do that, Sloane."

She wouldn't push. If he couldn't tell her because of his job... "Let's eat our ice cream and go back to the condo. I have every movie channel there is on my plan there. Let's order a pizza and watch action flicks until we're sick of them."

"I thought most of you ladies liked romantic comedies."

She shook her head. "I like action adventure. Give me a *Die Hard* movie or a scary one, and I'm happy."

He grinned. "I should have known."

"It'll be a first for you, won't it? Taking a day to do nothing but sit in front of the tube and watch other guys run around with guns. You can pick apart their technique and tell me everything they do wrong."

"Yeah, it will. I don't watch much television."

By the time they got back to the apartment he seemed more relaxed. Halfway through the first movie she ordered the pizza. They laughed together at John McClane's comedic asides during the first movie.

The undercurrent of awareness that seemed to bounce back and forth between them went into high alert when he rested his hand on her bare thigh. Her breath became labored and her throat dry, and she wanted to guide his hand higher, to where she wanted to be touched, and laced her fingers with his to keep from doing so.

She'd known Reed for three years and he'd trampled her heart. She'd only known Connor for five days. Heartbreak and caution kept her from taking the next impulsive step.

They chose *Jack Reacher* to watch next while they snacked on the pizza and drank sweet iced tea.

By the third movie she was curled tight against his side and he was resting his hand on her hip. The sexual awareness thrummed between them like the vibration from a stereo with the bass turned up.

"We could make out like we were back in high school," he breathed against her ear, making her shiver.

"My brothers never let me out of their sight in high school. So I never got to do that." Her throat felt thick with the heavy beat of her heart. She pressed a palm against his cheek, exploring the texture of his beard. "I'm so glad they're not here right now."

Connor laughed. "I am too," he said with feeling and kissed her.

All she could think as he eased her down on the couch was she'd never wanted a man inside her as much as she wanted him. It was a physical ache. He smelled of pizza and bug repellent and him. And he tasted of sweet iced tea and need as their lips and tongues dueled in a feverish quest for more.

His heart thudded against her as heavily as her own. She ran her hands beneath his shirt and up his broad back. The large couch was still too narrow for them to be completely comfortable, but when Connor's body covered hers, she couldn't resist the need to tilt her hips up in welcome.

His phone rang, playing the Marine Corps hymn, and he groaned and raised his head.

"That's Dad. He never calls unless it's important." He slipped his phone out of his back pocket and swiped the front while he continued to lie tantalizingly close. After he hung up he said, "The truck's got a flat and I have to pick him up at the tire place. They're going to have to put in a new rear axle, and he's going to have to leave it overnight. He's already closed up and there's no one at the nursery to pick him up or give him a ride."

Connor caught the tips of her fingers and drew her to her feet. "Come over to Dad's and we'll swim and grill out."

She shook her head. "I've had too much pizza. And we'd both be drooling every time we looked at each other..." Her cheeks heated. "I planned to ask you to have dinner here tomorrow night after we finish the scuba lesson."

"You cook?"

"I'm Italian. Of course I cook. It would be a travesty if I didn't."

He grinned, and she decided he was just too attractive to resist.

"I like to make my red sauce from scratch, and that takes a little time. I'll need to run to the market and do some shopping in preparation. Do you have a favorite dish you'd like me to fix?"

"I haven't met an Italian dish I didn't like."

She studied him. "I could take that the wrong way and be very pissed."

He chuckled. "No double entendre intended, I promise."

She smiled to let him know she was teasing. "Good answer." She patted his chest, aware every moment of the muscle beneath his shirt.

He drew her close. "Thank you for today, Sloane."

She nestled in close and rested her head against his chest. He cupped the back of her head then massaged the back of her neck. He even did that right.

"We both needed a day to relax and just be," she murmured.

"Yeah, I think so too."

She tilted her head back to look up at him. She wanted to ask him to stay, to lead him up the stairs to her room and make long, slow love to him. She ached with need.

His brown eyes looked dark as cocoa. He cupped her face in his hands and took her lips with a tenderness that had tears stinging her eyes.

"Call me in the morning when you know what time you'd like me to come over."

"I will." He brushed her lips with a kiss, then came back for more. "Gotta go. He'll be waiting."

Thrilled by his reluctance to release her, she smiled. "I'll make something special for dessert for tomorrow night," she said as she walked him to the door.

"I can tell you what I'd like," he teased.

She wanted the same thing. She just needed to learn to throw caution to the wind. As she stood at the door and watched him walk to his car, she wished she could rewind the last ten minutes and give in to temptation. But then his phone would have rung at just the wrong moment...probably.

CHAPTER 9

MOISTURE FROM AN early morning shower hung in the air and gave it just a touch of a nip. Wearing running shorts and a sleeveless T-shirt, Connor ignored the brief chill. He'd warm up soon enough when he started to run.

Standing on the front porch, he gripped the wooden porch rail and went through his normal stretching routine. His right knee gave him a brief twinge, but he ignored it. He'd begun to notice some wear and tear on his body in the past six months or so.

They all sustained injuries now and then. He'd had a couple of broken bones and some other more serious nicks, but he kept in shape and addressed the issues if they persisted. The knee thing was just a pinch now and then.

He turned as Toby stepped outside, a cup of coffee gripped in his hand.

"When's Sloane coming over?"

"Around nine."

"You'll need to pick up some sugar for sweet tea and something for lunch and dinner."

"I've had the tanks topped off. I'll do some shopping this morning on the way back from the dive shop." He paused. "I'll be eating at Sloane's place tonight. She's going to fix something Italian."

"You can bring her out to the nursery to look around before

you pick up the tanks, if you like. Let her find something she likes for her apartment. She does live in an apartment, doesn't she?"

"I don't know, but I'll ask."

"Most women like flowers." Toby wandered over and hiked a hip on porch railing. "After I opened the nursery, I was forever bringing home some of the newer plants to your mom. She fussed over them, fed them. She put in the flowerbeds all around the house. Even around the mailbox."

"I noticed."

"It was her idea for us to go into business when I retired."

Connor was surprised. "It was?"

"Yeah, she said I'd drive her crazy if I didn't have something to do."

He could definitely see that. He'd never heard his father talk so much. Mostly they communicated in grunts and nods.

"Have you decided what you want to do if you leave the teams?"

"Yeah. I have some ideas. I know I want to go back to school."

Toby nodded. "What would you focus on?"

"Engineering."

"You have the math skills, took calculus and all, and you've almost finished the business degree."

"Two more classes. I'll finish those while I'm cycling out."

On campus he'd be old enough to be some of the students' dad. The thought almost sent him into memories he didn't want to revisit, so he shut off the murmurings.

It would be an adjustment to leave the teams. Painful, probably. And he'd miss his teammates, but some of them were moving on too. There was life after the SEALs. He just needed to make up his mind what he wanted his life to look like moving on and aim for it. That's what his training demanded. Set a goal and work toward it with everything he had.

"How did you cope getting out of the Marines, Dad?"

"The same way I did while I was in. I kept my eye on what was important—keeping your mother happy and paying the bills.

The big difference was I didn't have to risk my life or dodge any bullets to do it." He sipped his coffee. "The last five years in weren't nearly as dangerous as the first twenty-five. My job then was making sure the younger guys were trained and outfitted to take over for me when I was gone. Important, sure, but not nearly as risky."

He cleared his throat. "In your job, there's always pressure, always risk, always danger. For twenty years, you've sacrificed everything for this job. You don't have to anymore."

Surprised by his vehemence, Connor straightened. "I didn't know you were concerned about my being in the teams."

"I've always been proud of what you do. Proud you felt called to serve your country." He paused for several moments. "But you haven't given yourself permission to have a life outside the teams, Connor. I know part of it is because of your grief, but I don't want you to go through the rest of your life alone. Everyone needs someone to come home to."

At Connor's silence, he continued.

"Have you told Sloane about any of it?"

"Just about Kate. We just met." And she was still recovering from a broken engagement and everything else that went along with it. "We're just getting to know each other."

"She doesn't strike me as the type for a casual relationship, Connor."

She wasn't. That thought gave him a moment's pause. "We don't know where this might go, Dad. But I enjoy her company."

"She's beautiful and funny, just as you said. I'd hate to see her hurt."

"That isn't my intention. But I'll be on one coast while she's on the other. I still have four months left of my enlistment. And I still haven't made a firm decision about whether I'll stay in or not. I've been doing things as though I'm going to muster out, I just haven't sent in the final paperwork."

"You have a few weeks to make up your mind."

He'd had enough of this heart-to-heart. What the hell was going on with his dad? "I'm going for my run, I'll be back in time to take you to work, and I'll bring Sloane over to the nursery before we hit the pool with the tanks."

"Okay."

He bounded down the stairs and cut across the drive to the road. He knew the route well. He kept his pace steady, warming his muscles, watching his breathing.

But concentrating on the run didn't keep his thoughts from running back through what his father had said. Sloane wasn't the kind to jump into bed indiscriminately. If she was, they'd have already tangled the sheets. She'd have been putting the move on him instead of talking about employment opportunities he might explore after the SEALs and watching movies with him. She was tempted. More than tempted. Her cheeks had reddened when he rested his palm on her thigh. When he kissed her it was like nothing he'd ever experienced before.

Her ex had treated her like shit, and Connor had no intention of following in his footsteps.

But he wanted her with a passion he'd never experienced before. Physically, mentally, emotionally—they clicked. And if he didn't get to experience making love with her, he'd regret it for a long, long time.

But he didn't have tomorrows to promise her. Not yet. And there would be twenty-five hundred miles between them when he left to go back to San Diego.

And why the hell was he thinking like this? They just met. They'd spent five days snorkeling, hiking, swimming together. And he found it impossible to keep his hands off her.

He needed to think about something else. Because he couldn't do a damn thing about any of the negative things standing in the way of...anything permanent.

He needed to deal with the feelings he'd crammed inside the box that kept leaking out at unexpected moments. The dreams that haunted him. The child in El Salvador who seemed to have gotten all tangled up with his Livy. Just thinking her name landed a boulder on his chest.

He couldn't go there. He wasn't ready.

SLOANE PUT THE finishing touches on the lasagna and put it in the refrigerator to bake later. She made the red sauce from scratch the night before, added the Italian sausage and ground chuck to it this morning, let it simmer, then built the lasagna with the cheeses and sauce.

She bought crusty Italian bread at her favorite bakery on the Island, but made the cannoli from scratch. A mixed green salad with carrots, cucumbers, black olives, green peppers, and crumbled feta cheese would go nicely with her special homemade raspberry vinaigrette dressing. Deciding to fix the salad when she returned from her scuba diving lesson, she set the bottle of vinaigrette in the refrigerator.

She told herself cooking for Connor would help relieve her nervousness about their upcoming evening, but it didn't. If she thought too long about it, she grew breathless. She hadn't felt this way about anyone, not even Reed—ever.

She had to maintain her cool. She would not embarrass herself. When it was time for her to go back to work in eleven days, she'd have to accept that this was just a short-term fling.

Connor had some big decisions to make, and whether or not to pursue a relationship wasn't one of them.

With those cautions ringing in her ears, she went into the bedroom to dress. If the undies she chose were some of her prettiest, she told herself it was because they were comfortable as well. She chose a wraparound skirt because she could wear it over her bathing suit later if she needed to. And while the cream-colored, short-sleeved shirt dipped a little lower in the front than normal, it was just as modest as her one-piece bathing suit.

She was standing at the door ready to walk out when the phone rang. Seeing that it was Bernie, she set aside her bags and swiped the screen.

"How are you doing?" Bernie asked as soon as she answered.

"Good." She took a seat on the stairs to the second floor. "How are you feeling?"

"I'm still sore, but I'm already healing. But I'm not telling Paul or the kids. I'm milking this for all it's worth. The kids are waiting on me hand and foot. Which is a real reversal. I could get used to this." She chuckled. "How is Mr. Hunk?"

"He's fine. Really fine. And his name is Connor."

"I remember. But he is a hunk. Wide shoulders, narrow hips, great biceps, beautiful brown eyes, and if I wasn't crazy about my own hunky hubby… How did things go the other day at his father's house?"

"We all three had dinner together. His father is a real sweetheart. Connor and I have spent the day together every day, and so far I've had two days of scuba, we went on a hike, and then watched movies. Connor's coming here for dinner tonight."

"What's for dessert?"

"Cannoli."

"I thought you might have him for dessert to break your dry spell and get a good look at his rusty nail."

"You have a one-track mind, Bernie. And I believe his nail will be as big and perfect as the rest of him. Not rusty at all." She fanned her hot face.

Bernie's whoop of laughter had her smiling.

"I want you to have a good rest while you're there, Sloane. Come back energized and ready to kick some butt. Let Connor relax you. Sex will do that for you."

"I can't jump into bed with a man on the forth date, Bernie." A big load of Catholic guilt kept interfering with those plans…or was it because she was chicken?

"You won't have a month to sit on the fence and let the good times pass you by, either."

She already knew that, but she'd never been casual about sex. She waited eight weeks before sleeping with Reed. Even longer with her college sweetheart. It was a big deal. She had to be sure.

"I'm going to practice more scuba diving today."

"Really?"

"Yes. Connor is challenging me to do things I've never done before."

"Wise man. That's just what you need. I'll overnight a copy of the Kama Sutra so you two can work on the positions together."

She was relentless. Sloane laughed. "You never give up."

"Neither do you. It's what makes us irresistible." Her tone changed. "You know I'm just teasing, don't you?"

"Yeah, I do."

"Don't do anything that doesn't feel right to you, Sloane. But my take on Connor is he's one of the good guys. He'd have to be really committed to stay in the Navy for twenty years."

Guilt gave her a pinch. She wished she could tell Bernie about him. "I'm sure he is, too."

"And be careful, okay?"

"I will. Connor knows what he's doing. I feel comfortable because I know he'll keep me safe underwater."

"Good. Call me. I'm about to pull my poor pitiful mom thing and get someone to fix me some coffee."

Sloane laughed. "Enjoy that while it lasts."

"I'm going to."

What would she do without Bernie? Her mother had been too busy blaming her for the breakup without realizing the cause was something she had no control over. She'd been too raw, too devastated to share the real reason with anyone. Without Bernie by her side…she'd have had no one.

And what was she going to do when she returned to work? Winning the case had taken the pressure off for a short while, but the partners' attitude toward her had damaged her trust in them as well as the relationships she used to have with some of the other lawyers in the firm. She would no longer stand for being their whipping girl. Life was too short to live like that.

She needed to do some thinking of her own.

The phone rang and, thinking it was Bernie again, she swiped the screen. "Did you forget something?"

"Sloane?"

Hearing Reed's voice at the other end of the line shot adrenaline through her system and stole her breath. How had he gotten through? Connor had blocked his number.

"Don't hang—."

She cut the call off. She didn't want or need to think about Reed. She was certain of that.

She went to recent calls and wrote down the number on a pad on the entrance table, then went to settings and blocked his number as Connor had done yesterday. After several deep breaths, she left the condo.

She concentrated on finding the house in Beaufort, but her mind was racing a mile a minute. She was over Reed. Had been for months now. She'd found a handsome, fantastic guy who could make her toes curl when he kissed her, and she was going to enjoy him. And she wasn't going to feel guilty for sleeping with him.

When she arrived at the house, Connor was sitting on the front porch steps. While she parked, he got to his feet. His long legs, muscular and tanned, snagged her attention when he came to greet her.

She gathered the bag of food she set aside for Toby and her swim gear from the back seat. He reached to take the bags from her.

"It's nice out here this early. That paper bag is for your father. It's dinner."

He opened the bag and breathed in the aroma. "Smells good. Thanks for thinking of him." He rested a hand against her waist as they climbed the steps. "He was thinking of you, too. He told me to bring you out to the nursery before we get started in the pool. He wants me to give you a tour."

They passed through the large living room, cozy and warm, and moved into the kitchen. She envied Toby the large island and six-burner gas stove. What she could do on that baby. "You can just put all that in the refrigerator. I've written directions on the top on a post-it."

Unloading the bag, he shoved everything in the refrigerator, and then turned to face her. He took her beach bag, set it on the counter and eased in close. With a bent index finger, he tipped her chin up so he could brush his lips against first one cheek, then the other, taking his time. When he finally reached her lips, her knees went jelly weak.

"I like this." He toyed with the tie at her waist that held the skirt in place.

Tingling heat settled low. No other man had made her wet by just kissing her.

"I have some errands I have to run, but I'd like to take some time for us first," he said, his tone husky.

If he took any more time she was going to die of sexual frustration. She leaned in against him and encountered solid evidence that he was suffering from something similar. Every word she'd preached to herself all the way here was drowned out by the hum that escaped her, sounding suspiciously like a purr. She toyed with the top button of his cotton shirt until she unfastened it, then the next.

Connor cupped her hips and pulled her tighter against him, his lips finding hers. Their tongues mated in a kiss that scorched away any lingering reservations.

"I know we've only known each other for a few days..." he murmured, his voice smoky.

When she pressed a kiss against the V of bare skin she had exposed, his voice fell away and he sucked in a breath.

"This will be another first for me," she said.

His eyes darkened as she unbuttoned another button.

She gave a squeak of surprise when he scooped her up, and she gripped his shirt. "You'll hurt your back."

"Not going to happen. You're not that heavy."

That was the first time he'd ever lied to her, but she decided not to hold it against him, because he was pulling a Rhett Butler—and didn't seem to be struggling while he was doing it, either.

He shoved the second door on the right open with his foot and stepped into a large bedroom decorated in sage green. He lowered her to the center of a queen-sized bed and took a step back to hastily finish unbuttoning his shirt. He started to peel it off his shoulders, and she sat up and threw out a hand. "Wait."

Dear God, he was beautiful. He'd worn dark T-shirts in the

pool both days, and it had clung to every masculine line of his torso. But with his shoulders and chest broad, muscular, and bare, and his skin smooth and tanned from being in the pool, she found it hard to drag her gaze away from him. His beard darkened the lower half of his face, giving him a dangerously seductive masculinity.

Before the hawk-like intensity in his dark eyes could dim, she said, "I just want to look at you for a second."

He grinned, slipped off the shirt and tossed it onto the dresser. "You're about to get a good look at the whole package, up close and personal. No pun intended."

She laughed, then toed off her slip-on canvas shoes and pushed them over the side of the bed.

He reached for the button at the waistband of his khaki shorts, and she tugged her T-shirt up and off and offered it to him. His eyes lasered in on the lacy white bra cupping her breasts as he tossed her shirt toward the dresser. She peeled the straps down her arms, reached behind to unfasten it, and dropped it over the side of the bed.

When he dropped his shorts and boxer briefs, she got a good look at how much she affected him, and her mouth went dry with anticipation and need.

She pulled the tie on her skirt.

Connor said, "Let me."

He unfolded the cotton fabric, spreading it open on either side of her. His attention settled on the tiny scrap of lace that matched the bra. His dark eyes seemed to look right through the garment as he ran the backs of his fingers from her navel down over that thin barrier, then slipped his fingers between her legs to caress the inside of one thigh.

The throb of need that erupted inside her took her breath. She bit her lip to hold back the whimper of need, and gripped the bedspread to help her resist the urgent need to move against his touch.

Connor braced a knee and hand on the bed and bent to press an openmouthed kiss with a bit of tongue just beneath her belly button while he worked her panties down. She was trembling as he drew them free of her feet and tossed them to the floor with the rest of their clothes.

He climbed up, covering her with his body, and when the firm heat of his erection rested against her intimately she caught her breath. Despite the raw sexuality of his caresses, his mouth took hers with a tenderness she wasn't expecting. She raised her hands to cup his face, the springy softness of his beard a texture in contrast to the softness of his lips.

The drugging sweetness of his kisses left her breathless and aching with need. His large hand cupped her breast while his lips trailed across the soft slope, then covered the nipple. She released a small sigh at the sensation he triggered as his tongue stroked and feathered the underside. Then he sucked, the pressure flatting her nipped against the roof of his mouth triggering delightful tendrils of sensation deep inside her.

It had been so long since she'd been touched, had wanted to be touched. Connor knew just where to stroke, kiss, and nibble. With every brush of his hand, every kiss, and the careful pressure of his fingertips, he built a wild, unfettered passion in her.

She loved the brush of his beard against her skin as his lips followed the shallow dip between her ribs, the curve of her belly, the inside of her thighs, tempting her, teasing her and driving her pleasure and anticipation higher.

She sat up to cup his face and draw his lips back to hers, the movement of his muscles tensing and releasing when she stroked his broad back, his muscular ribs, his washboard abs. He pressed a condom in her palm, and she quickly sheathed him, for a moment cupping his erection, gripping the hard heat of him. The husky tone of his deep voice as he urged her to guide him home was as physical as a kiss.

Then he was inside her, thrusting deep, hitting the spot that drove her need higher with every movement. Her orgasm rushed up and over her like a runaway locomotive, and her hips jerked with the intensity of the contractions.

Connor had never seen anything as beautiful as Sloane tipping over the edge.

He paused a moment to let her recover, then began to move again. Her body gripped him like a velvet glove, beckoning his own release closer and closer. Each time her hips rose to accept him, he had to fight against his release while he waited for her to find hers again. He reached between their bodies and found her with his fingers, and her body bowed, clamping around him, wrecking the tenuous hold he had on his control. He lost his rhythm, his thrusts turning choppy and quick. He groaned aloud as eight months of celibacy reached critical mass, and he pitched over into bliss.

Sloane's heart hammered against him and her breath was warm against his neck. He turned his head to kiss her, then rolled to one side and gathered her close against him. When he looped a long strand of hair behind her ear, she smiled.

"It's been a long sixteen months," she murmured, kissed his bare shoulder, and traced a long, thin scar across his upper arm with her fingertip, then kissed it.

He reciprocated by tipping her face up to kiss her lips. "A long eight months for me. I've been in and out of the country and training."

"I haven't really had the desire to date until now."

He understood all too well what it was like to have a relationship implode. "Recovering from a relationship that's ended is tough."

"Yes. And I've never been one to use sex as a release valve."

"I've been guilty of that, and it never works out like people think it will." He couldn't believe he just said that to her.

Her tawny eyes settled on his face while she brushed his short hair back to its normal order. "We ladies just go out and buy a big Vance or a bigger Vincent to keep us company."

He raised a brow, laughter glittering in his dark eyes. "You name your sex toys."

"Of course. You have to have something to call them during the finale."

He laughed.

She ran a finger down his cheek. "I'm not just ending a dry spell with you, Connor."

He tangled his fingers with hers. "I didn't think you were."

"I've never done anything like this before. Never allowed myself to reach for what I want without analyzing it to death."

"I'm glad you did. This thing we have between us…is beyond my experience."

"Mine, too. I'd like us to stay friends, Connor. Even after this is over. I don't want to feel like this didn't matter."

He wasn't sure where they were going. It was too soon. But friends seemed a bit tame to describe what they had here. Friends didn't lust after each other like teenagers.

She moved to curl against his side. "We have nine days before I go home."

He suddenly realized she was playing the role he usually assumed, cautioning him that she wouldn't be around in a few days. And finding himself on the other side of things, feeling the disappointment and regret, gave him a hard emotional rap.

He needed more than a few days with Sloane. Now they'd entered the mating dance and he'd gotten a taste of her, he wanted more.

"I need to go take care of something. I'll be right back."

He rose to dispose of the condom down the toilet and wash his hands. While standing in the bathroom doorway, he paused to run his gaze over every generous curve of her body. Her breasts were full and round, her waist tiny compared to the curve of her hip. He was pleased to notice how her nipples puckered at his interest.

He forced his thoughts to something else. Jesus, he wanted her all over again. "Do you live in a house or an apartment?"

"An apartment."

"How big an apartment?" He slipped in snuggled her close again.

"A two-bedroom close to work."

"Do you have a balcony?" Using his fingertips, he caressed the smooth curve of her shoulder and trailed his touch over her collarbone.

Her throat moved as she swallowed. "Yes, a very small one. Why?" She reached up and traced the tattoo on his wrist.

If she asked about the tattoo, he'd have to explain, but he didn't want to. He rushed on before she could question him about it. "I was thinking about the plant Dad wants to give you. Just trying to get some ideas about the amount of room you have."

"You sound as though you're certain he'll give me a plant."

"It's his thing. He likes you a lot, and besides that you've made him food. He'll want to give you something live to thank you."

"That's really sweet. If it's small, I have several places I can put it."

"I was thinking of something that would suit you better than a bouquet."

Her brows rose, a look of interest on her face.

"We'll talk more about it when we get out to the nursery. We can get under the covers," he suggested.

"I like the view just fine from here." She ran a hand over his shoulder, then down over his chest.

Urging her closer, he pressed his lips to her shoulder and breathed in the vanilla scent on her skin. "I don't stop wanting you. I just distract myself with other things to keep from thinking about being inside you. That's the way it's been since I first laid eyes on you."

Her gold-tinted eyes fastened on his face, cheeks heated with desire as she licked her lips, her breath coming faster. "Then come inside me again. I'm already wet for you." At her invitation, spoken in that soft, husky voice, he went painfully hard in an instant. He reached for a condom and covered himself.

When she rolled onto her back, he followed and slipped inside her. She made a soft sound, a cross between a catch of breath and a hum of pleasure. He bent his head to place an openmouthed kiss beneath her ear. Then along her jaw.

She shivered in response and cupped his naked buttocks. When she scraped her teeth playfully along his shoulder, he groaned. Jesus, if she kept that up he wasn't going to last even a full minute.

He thrust deep, seating himself tightly inside her, the warmth of her body a tempting torment. He kissed her with hungry pleasure. When she began moving beneath him, he pulled back to thrust again and again in quick, deep strokes, sealing their bodies together until they rocked the bed.

Her hands caressed and massaged at the same time, urging him on. He'd had his share of lovers, but she was so responsive to his every move, as hungry for him as he was for her.

She lightly raked her nails down his back. The sensation drove his need to DEFCON One in a split second.

"Sloane," her name came out a strangled gasp.

"Oh, God. You feel so good," she breathed.

Those few words set him off. His release raged through him, seeming to go on forever. When his breathing leveled out, he raised his head to look down at her. Her cheeks glowed, and her pupils were so large that only a narrow ring of gold remained.

Had he been physically able, he'd have taken her all over again.

Jesus, he was in trouble.

CHAPTER 10

T HE SMELL OF fertilizer and blooming flowers blended on the sluggish breeze as Sloane got out of the car and tucked her purse strap over her shoulder.

Connor caught her hand as they strolled across the gravel parking lot to the main office. Even that casual contact had her heart drumming. A passion like this couldn't sustain itself forever, but she could—and would—enjoy it for the next nine days. Now she knew what she was missing, she wished she'd slept with him that first night.

They passed row after row of trees planted with military precision across several acres of land on the drive up, but here rows of greenhouses stretched alongside the main structure. A pebbled patio curved around the exterior of the office and branched out into sidewalks that stretched out on either side, and creative displays using some of the available plants were set up along the borders while a large fountain trickled in the sunniest area of the patio. The main building squatted beneath the shade of a huge Magnolia tree.

"One day I'd like to buy a house and have a Magnolia tree in my yard," she commented.

"They're nice trees, but they shed their leaves, and it's a chore to rake them up."

"But they bloom beautifully, and the blossoms smell wonderful."

"They take a long time to get established and to bloom, though. Up to eight years."

"Really? So long?"

"Yeah. This one was already here when Dad built the place." He opened the door for her.

Sloane smiled as she eyed the interior. The structure was long, with wide wooden beams, and set up like a country store, with shelves along the walls and displays set up in the center aisle.

"Uh-oh. I've seen that look before."

"What look?"

"The look of an avid shopper."

"Actually all you're seeing is a look of interest, because I'm not a gardener, and I don't have a clue about any of this. It's just the country store ambiance." She narrowed her eyes at him. "And if we were in the a sporting goods store looking at fishing equipment, tents, camp stoves, and all that, what kind of look would be on your face?"

He grinned. "Guilty. Why don't you look around while I go find Dad?"

"Okay."

Other people milled around the store, seeming to know exactly what they needed.

She wandered down one of the aisles and studied the supplies on the shelves. Flower pots, hanging baskets, bird feeders, bird food, potting soil, plant food, fertilizer, peat moss, sand, tools, hoses, wind chimes, all sorts of knickknacks to put in the yard, and several types of powder and spray to protect plants from insects. How could anyone have a clue what they needed?

She paused by a five-foot-wide magazine rack with books on how to build a deck, how to plant vegetables, and several other germane topics. She was thumbing through one of them when Connor returned.

"He's out back in one of the greenhouses."

She replaced the book on the rack and walked with him around the back of the building.

Inside the greenhouse, huge fans at either end stirred the air, keeping the temperature moderate. Sprinkler systems hung over tables that supported numerous pots of flowers.

Toby smiled when he saw her, his gloved hands in a large pot "Hi. Glad you could come by."

"Thanks. This is an impressive business you've got here."

"It keeps me busy. Come on over and see what I'm doing."

She moved close to the table, which had sides built up to trap any dirt or debris. At one corner, clippings lay gathered.

"I've put sand, clay and peat moss together in this mix. Connor says you like Magnolias."

"They're lovely. And when I have a house, I'll plant one."

"Well, even the smallest Magnolia can grow between eight and twenty feet, so a balcony garden won't sustain it. But I have something that smells just as good, and I'm potting it for you. You can keep it on your balcony, and it will perfume the air throughout spring and summer."

"You don't have to do that."

"I know, but," he leaned close, "if you're going to keep Connor occupied while I'm busy, you deserve some kind of compensation."

Her face flashed hot. If he knew how they'd occupied each other earlier—"What kind of plant is it?"

"It's a dwarf gardenia radicans." He raised a plastic pot from the floor to sit on the table. "It stays green year-round, only grows about three feet tall, blooms all spring and summer, and puts out a wonderful fragrance. And it doesn't take much effort to care for. I'm potting two for you. You can put them on either side of your balcony door, and if you leave the door open, the scent will come right into the apartment."

She breathed in the fragrance of the small white blossoms. "It smells wonderful, and it's really sweet of you."

He smiled. "When you buy that house, come back and get your Magnolia."

She laughed. "Sold."

"So, you've already been looking for a house?"

"Yes, I've done some looking...actually, a lot of looking and dreaming...and I have a nest egg saved for a down payment." She'd backed off recently, due to her employment issues, but when she returned to Charleston, she was going to send her resume to every big firm in the area.

"What kind of house are you interested in?"

"Yours is gorgeous. And I love the style. But I don't need anything quite as big for just me."

"Someday it might not be just you."

That gave her heart a squeeze. But she couldn't count on it. "Maybe, but I can't depend on someday, so I'm going to live my dreams, and maybe I'll find someone who wants to share them with me."

Toby shot a look toward his son. "Whoever they may be won't just drop out of the sky. You have to put yourself out there. Had I not met Marian standing in line at the movies and introduced myself, Connor wouldn't be here."

Sloane bit her bottom lip and refused to look at Connor. The warmth of his body radiated against her back, and when he laid his hand on her shoulder, she touched his fingers.

Toby glanced up at her, then went back to what he was doing, a slight smile curving his mouth.

She reached to touch one of the blossoms and inhaled the fragrance again. "You'd better tell me how to take care of these so I don't kill them. What kind of sun, and how much water, and I noticed some plant food, but I have no idea what kind to buy." And she'd pay for the pots and other materials at least.

He went through everything she needed to do to keep the plants healthy, then he and Connor loaded the two heavy pots into a high-sided wagon.

"Take my truck so you can haul these to the house. You can take them to Sloane's this evening." Toby held out his keys, and Connor gave him the car keys in exchange.

"I'm glad you came, Sloane."

He extended his hand and she stepped past it to hug him. "Thank you."

"Sloane left dinner for you in the refrigerator." Connor said. "It's enough for two."

Toby's eyebrows rose.

Before he could thank her, she said, "When you're cooking it's easy to throw in a few extra tomatoes and a little more pasta. I hope you'll enjoy it."

"Thanks. I'm sure I will."

Connor pulled the wagon to the parking lot. "We have one more stop to make before we go back to the house."

The sun was higher and the air still. "You talked it over with your dad about what kind of plant I'd like."

"The other night I noticed you liked the jasmine and clematis that Mom planted, and you commented on the Magnolia. So we picked something that has a strong, sweet fragrance that would also thrive on your balcony without taking up too much room." He lowered the truck's bent tailgate and loaded the two pots.

"It was very thoughtful. Thank you. But I want to pay for at least half the cost."

Connor shook his head. "Dad got free labor out of me the first two days I was here, and you've thanked him with a meal he'll enjoy. And you've already thanked me." He shot her a smile. "But you can do it again any time you like."

Heat touched her cheeks even as her body quickened at the suggestion. Connor opened the truck door for her, offering her a hand up. Once she was settled he said, "I'll be right back. Need to return the garden wagon to the office."

She tracked him as he strode back to the office and parked the wagon. He was so careful about everything he said, other than the fact that he wanted her. He kept everything on the surface. Like the tattoo on his wrist. Who was Olivia? An old flame? A younger sister? Someone important, for certain. Maybe she'd find an opportunity to ask him later, over dinner.

Or should she? She was only a temporary lover. And it wasn't her business. The thought gave her a hard pinch.

BENEATH THE WATER, the hollow sound of each breath he released was as familiar as his own footsteps. He watched Sloane as she sat on the bottom of the pool and regulated her breathing.

He remembered drownproofing during BUD/S. One of the guys hadn't quite made it to the surface and almost drowned.

How many missions had he been on where they infiltrated the area from the water? Twenty? Twenty-five? Adding in training missions brought the count up to a hundred times at least. He'd always thrived on the challenge.

But this wasn't supposed to be a real challenge. It was supposed to be something fun for Sloane. And he didn't get that from her. She was doing it more to please him than because she wanted to.

She wouldn't back down from this any more than she would from her ex and the partners of her law firm.

But she had nothing to prove to him, and apparently he needed to make that clear. If scuba wasn't her cup of tea, it was okay. Because if something happened to her—The idea gave his insides a twist. The chances were slim, but they were real. For all the pleasure of scuba diving, there was an edge of danger to it too. Something that hounded most everything he and his teammates did.

Behind her mask, her eyes were closed. Her body looked relaxed, and her hands rested on her thighs. When he touched her wrist, she startled and her tawny eyes sprang open.

Using the hand signals he'd taught her, he motioned for her to surface.

She kicked off from the bottom of the twelve-foot depth and turned to paddle to the steps leading down into the pool.

She pulled the mouthpiece free, perched on the steps on one hip, and pushed the facemask atop her head.

He joined her. "You're doing really well."

"But?"

"If this is as far as you want to go with it, it's fine. You've experienced what it's like to use the tanks, and you've been a quick study with everything I've taught you."

She focused on her flippers as she moved them in the water. "It's—a little claustrophobic looking up and seeing the water overhead."

"Is that what the meditation is for?"

"Yes, to calm me. It helps with my breathing, too."

"That's a good idea. But once you're in the ocean, there will be other things to focus on besides looking up. But if you don't want to try it, it's okay."

"You'll be with me. I trust you to keep me safe."

The tightness in his stomach loosened. "We'll practice a couple more times in the pool before we go out. And Dad will come along to spot us one day this coming week."

"Okay."

As he dressed to follow her home for dinner, he thought about the trust he read in her eyes, her expression. He couldn't protect her from being hurt after they parted. He couldn't promise her more than these few days. But he wanted to. That thought sent a short burst of panic through him. He hadn't done a bang-up job as a husband or a boyfriend. And the teams were only part of why.

If he let Sloane down... He didn't want to think about it.

SLOANE COULD REALLY cook. The lasagna was delicious, the salad dressing a surprise, and the bread fresh. She owned that she hadn't baked it or the dessert, but it didn't matter. The fact that she could have if she had the time was impressive enough.

He could tell she really enjoyed cooking from the way she served it. The salad had curls of carrot to garnish it, shaped like a flower. She'd blended seasoned olive oil to dip the bread in. The lasagna looked like it should be in a cooking magazine. And he even liked the wine, though he wasn't a wine drinker.

They should have created an herb garden for her instead of the potted shrubs for her balcony. He might do it anyway before she left.

When he pushed his chair back from the table, he was stuffed. "I feel like I just had a meal at a five-star restaurant. If you ever decide to give up the law, you could open your own restaurant."

The way she smiled told him she was pleased by the compliment.

"Thank you. We can clear the table later. I thought we could take a walk on the beach until our food has settled," she suggested. "We can have dessert and coffee when we get back."

"I'm up for that."

When they arrived at the beach, the sun had already kissed the horizon good night and was nodding off fast, while purplish blue clouds hovered over the water, promising another storm out at sea.

The crowds who would have littered the sand had left, and only small clusters of people remained, either sitting watching the tide, or walking the beach close to the water.

A young girl of six or seven danced in a puddle of water left behind by the tide. Her hair caught the last rays of reflective light as the clouds shifted, giving the crown of her head a red-gold halo. A woman called to her, and she rushed up the sand to join her, grabbing the woman's hand.

Against Connor's will, his attention was drawn to the woman and girl as they followed them down the beach. The failing light turned their forms into silhouettes against the pale sand. His heart thundered in his ears, and his breath came in shallow gasps. Anxiety ripped through him, and he had the urge to run down the beach after them.

Sloane's voice sounded muffled, but reached him. "I used to love to sit out on my grandmother's porch and watch it storm. She had this old-fashioned metal glider, and I'd bundle up in it with a blanket and pillow. It never occurred to me or my grandmother that I would have been electrocuted if lightning struck while I was sitting there."

He dragged in a breath to steady himself. His hearing cleared. "We played baseball in the rain with an aluminum bat. When you're kids, you don't worry about what could happen, you just live in the moment."

He was grateful when she changed the subject.

"Any of your grandparents still living?" she asked.

"Yeah. My mom's parents are still alive. And she has a brother who lives in Seattle. I've been up to see him and his family. Dad has two sisters, and we've been to Tennessee to see them and their families. But when families are spaced out it's hard to keep in touch or stay close." And he had lost touch with so many because of his job. "Tell me about your family."

"That might take all night. We have a large family."

"Just hit the highlights."

"There's my grandparents, who are both in their mid-seventies. He was a civil engineer and she was a teacher. They still live alone, unassisted. They had six children, so I have numerous aunts and uncles and cousins, and then they all have families. We have somewhere between twenty-five to thirty people for Christmas at my grandparents' house. Mostly outside if the weather permits. They live in Savannah."

Thirty people. Jesus. "That's quite a clan."

"Yeah. It's a little wild with all the adults and the kids. Have you ever thought about marriage?"

There was the question he'd been dreading. "Yeah. I was married for almost six years. We divorced five years ago."

"I'm sorry, Connor."

"She's remarried and has a little boy." His throat ached. "He's two. We still stay in touch."

"It's good you've stayed friends."

"She deserves to be happy." He didn't know what he deserved after the way he behaved afterward... That was part of the problem. That and the PTSD dogging him right now. The guilt still ate at him. He brutally tamped down the swell of pain and grief that threatened to rise.

She remained silent, though she slipped an arm through his and leaned against him. He wasn't surprised by the offer of comfort. She was a giver. Like Cynthia.

She deserved better. He should have spent more time thinking this thing through instead of just grabbing for what he wanted.

CHAPTER 11

T HEY HAD BARELY gotten in the door when Connor said, "I have to shove off, Sloane."

His words didn't entirely surprise her. She'd felt his distance from the moment she asked about his marital status.

She had just started to know him a little, but had barely scratched the surface. She studied his handsome features, remembering how his beard felt against her skin, how he felt as he moved inside her.

Her throat felt tight. If he walked away now, she'd probably never see him again. "Okay." The one word came out almost a whisper.

"Thanks for dinner."

"Sure."

He stepped toward her, then hesitated. "I'll call you tomorrow."

She didn't believe he would. The words *don't go* pushed against her teeth. *Tell me what I did, what I said.* She couldn't be that clingy, vulnerable woman any more than he'd want her to be. She wouldn't let him make her that woman. She clenched a fist against the spot just beneath her breastbone where a physical pain had set in.

He brushed a kiss across her lips, then turned to the door.

She had to say something. "I think you deserve to be happy

too, Connor."

He hesitated, his hand upon the doorknob. He half turned, presenting his profile, as though he would make some reply, but then jerked open the door and stepped into the night.

Her legs turned to jelly, and she gripped the back of one of the dining room chairs and lowered herself into it. How could one question cause him to react this way?

Unless he was still in love with his wife. Still grieving her loss. Grieving her having a child with another man.

But he'd seemed sincere when he said she deserved to be happy.

But he didn't believe he did. Why?

The doorbell rang, and she gave a sigh of relief. Surely they could talk this through.

She opened the door and froze. Reed. His blond hair looked silver under the porch light. His classic features, straight, narrow nose, high brow ridge, and strong jaw seemed less defined, and he'd gained weight since she last saw him. She moved to shut the door, but he caught the edge with his hand. "I just want to talk, Sloane. I've been calling for days."

"Let go of the door. If I wanted to talk, I'd have answered the phone." She jerked at the door to try and wrench it from his grasp.

He shoved it open, and she staggered back against the wall, going down on one knee. She caught the edge of the kitchen door facing to keep from falling forward.

He gripped her arm to help her stand and she jerked away, tears close. "Don't touch me."

"If you'd be reasonable that wouldn't have happened."

Reasonable! *Reasonable?* She eased over to the entry table and grasped the car keys to use as a weapon if she needed to. "I see you're still blaming other people for your mistakes."

He waltzed into the dining area and eyed the dishes. "Who was the asshole you had over for dinner?"

"The only asshole I see is the one standing in front of me."

Reed raked his dark blond hair back from his forehead and

drew a deep breath. "I just want to talk, Sloane."

"We don't have anything to talk about."

"I feel that we do."

His expression settled into lines of contrition as fake as his capped teeth. What had she ever seen in him?

"I want to apologize to you and see if we can at least be friends again."

Friends? "No. I don't want to be *friends*. I don't want you anywhere near me. I want you to leave." She twisted the knob and held the door open.

"Look, I know things went a little too far with us."

"Too far in terms of a three-year involvement, or too far when you tried to get me fired and take over my job?"

"I want to come back to the firm, Sloane. Johnson won't let me as long as there's bad blood between us."

"I don't give a shit about you, Reed. Whatever we had ended the day you left. I don't even care how many women you fucked while we were engaged. And it was certainly completely over when I had to be tested to make sure you didn't give me some kind of lingering plague."

His jaw tensed. "Maybe if you'd given me more of your time than you gave the job..."

She laughed. "You didn't mind that I was paying most of the bills while you freeloaded off of me at the apartment."

"I had loans to pay off."

"Yes, so we could buy a house when we got married. And now you have them paid off, you're free to do what you like. So go do it away from me."

"I want to come back to H, C and J."

"I don't care what you want, Reed."

His jaw pulsed.

"You're not a child, though you behave like one," she snapped. "Grow up. Sometimes we can't have what we want. But that's not the problem, is it? You've always gotten what you wanted. And I kept you from taking it all, didn't I?"

"I'll still get it. You'll eventually leave the firm."

"And eventually someone there will figure out that you're a backstabbing son of a bitch. Your behavior was too low for there to *ever* be any kind of trust between us. And there are others there who witnessed it. Now leave."

And she'd make sure he couldn't get anywhere near her clients. She'd take them with her if she could. "When did you start hating me, Reed? When I worked seventy-hour weeks and still came home to cook your dinner and do your laundry, and have sex with you whenever you wanted it? Or when I got the Olson case? Is your ego really that fragile?"

He stormed past her onto the concrete porch. "Get used to seeing me. I'll be there at H,C & J when you get back to work."

She slammed the door behind him and locked it.

Trembling with anger and nerves, she stumbled into the living room and sat down on the couch.

She hadn't seen him in over a year. Had hoped never to see him again. Hadn't expected him to be so coldly aggressive toward her. It was he who had ended things, blaming it on her inability to have children. He left her confused, devastated, and feeling like less than a woman because of her sterility and his unfaithfulness.

And now he was wedging himself back into the firm. She'd have to cover her ass even more thoroughly than she had the past year. She needed to change the locks on her office door. Buy a nanny cam to monitor her office for security.

She didn't think she could stand this. Tears welled, and she pressed her palms against her eyes.

What hold did he have over Johnson that would force the man to take him back? As good as Reed was with clients, he was only a mediocre lawyer. She had expected him to improve with experience, but he'd been too busy screwing interns and riding on the other attorneys' coattails, including hers.

She'd been a fool. She allowed him to take advantage in every way because she believed he loved her. Why hadn't she recognized his selfishness? He always wanted her attention on him while they were at home, and was resentful if she brought work home. So she spent more time at the office. Time he spent screwing other women.

He wasn't going to make this about her shortcomings. Never again would she let a man tear her down so he could feel better about himself.

It was time to work on her resume now and start sending it out to all the major corporate law offices in Charleston she hadn't already queried.

But first she'd call Clay Johnson and make certain he was thinking about taking Reed back. It would be just like Reed to stir a pot with nothing in it, hoping she'd walk away without a struggle.

Her eyes fell on the remnants of the meal she shared with Connor earlier, and she fended off a quick-sharp pain. It seemed her ability to judge a man's character hadn't improved in the past year.

Time to clean up the mess. She found the menial task of loading the dishwasher and washing the pots and pans calming. Once finished, she poured another glass of wine and retrieved her computer from the bedroom. She made a list of questions she wanted to ask her boss concerning Reed's hiring so she'd be able to address her concerns about working with him.

With Reed it was always someone else's fault. It was her fault he slept around because she didn't give him enough attention. It was always the fault of one of the other lawyers when a contract didn't go through or there was a mistake on a filed document. Never his own.

Why hadn't she seen that long ago? Why had she been so blinded by his charm and humor?

Had she been blinded by Connor's, too? Was he still married? Was it guilt that kicked him out of the apartment and had him hurrying away? Would Toby allow him to string her along and not say anything?

She couldn't see him standing by and allowing his son to commit adultery.

So, Connor wasn't ready to share anything personal with her. She'd rolled right into a stranger's bed and expected him to respect and trust her.

She covered her face to try and block out the moments they shared earlier this morning.

How cliché was it that she'd become a one-night stand?

And it was her own damn fault.

But she couldn't think about that now. It hurt too much.

She pulled up her resume, then decided to call Bernie.

"Hey, how are things going?" Bernie asked.

"Not so well. Connor and I had dinner and everything was fine. We went for a walk on the beach, and I asked him if he'd ever been tempted by marriage. He told me he's been divorced for five years, was married for six. But after that, as soon as we got back to the condo, he left."

"Did he say why?"

"No. Just that he needed to leave."

Bernie remained silent for a beat...then two.

"That isn't all of it. As soon as he left, Reed showed up at the door and shoved his way in." She wouldn't tell Bernie how he knocked her down, then blamed her for it. It would only upset her, and she needed to rest and recover so they'd both be in fighting form. "He claims that Johnson is planning to hire him back."

"No way." Bernie's voice rose with shock.

"Yeah. I think he is. I'm going to call in the morning and discuss it with him."

She could practically see Bernie shaking her head when she said, "The guy has cost him a lawsuit and bad publicity. Why would he hire him back?"

"I've been thinking about that. I think Reed may have something on him, something personal that Johnson doesn't want exposed. And Reed would have no compunction at all about using it to get what he wants."

"After what he tried to pull on you, I don't doubt it. You're so much better off without that asshole, Sloane."

"I thank God every day that I didn't marry him." She took a deep breath. "I'm going to update my resume, Bernie. I think you need to do the same. I'm going to start applying to other firms right away."

"Mine's ready to go."

"I'll email you the addresses of the ones I apply to so you can do the same. You're my right hand, and I don't want to have to break in another administrative assistant. You know the law as well as I do, so I'm hoping they'll want us both."

"And if this doesn't work?"

"I'll start my own firm. I have a little money put aside."

"That was supposed to be for your house, Sloane."

"If I can get an office with an apartment above it, it will kill two birds with one stone. I'll have one payment instead of two."

"You've been thinking about this for a while."

"Ever since the lawsuit." She took a sip of her wine and wished it was something stronger. "With Reed there, we'll need to up our security to protect the integrity of our files. If Johnson corroborates what Reed said, I'll buy a couple of nanny cams to place in your office and mine, and have new locks installed on our file cabinets. I've been concerned someone might get into our files and plant something, or conveniently lose something important."

"It's going to be okay, Sloane."

If Reed came back on board, it wouldn't. She had hoped to have a few weeks to recover from the year from hell. Her eyes stung. "I sound awfully paranoid, don't I?"

"With reason. Johnson breathed down your neck throughout the whole trial, waiting to pounce. I saw it, and so did other people in the office."

"His name may be last on the letterhead, but he holds the controlling interest in the firm. And no one else in the firm would ever have the resources to buck him. If he wants Reed, he'll get him." She rubbed at the headache starting to pound at her temples. "I can't work with him, Bernie."

"I know. But I can, and I can keep an eye on him until you find a place, Sloane."

She shook her head even though Bernie couldn't see it. "He'd never go for that, and I wouldn't either."

There was a beat of silence.

"I made love with Connor." The words just seemed to come out of her mouth without her control.

Bernie paused a moment. "Before he left."

"Earlier this morning."

"And he suddenly gave you the cold shoulder tonight?"

"Yeah."

Bernie's silence stretched. "I should have never opened my big mouth and encouraged you to take the leap."

"That isn't why I did it, Bernie. I did it because I wanted to. It's been over a year since I've been held, touched. I wanted him. He wanted me just as much. I know I wasn't the only one feeling it."

"Maybe he'll call tomorrow and talk to you about what was bothering him."

She doubted it. It wasn't anything she had done. There was something going on with him. She was tired of moody, secretive assholes.

"He'd be a fool to walk away just when the two of you were getting to know each other."

"He's got four months left to serve in the Navy. And I knew this was only going to be a short-term thing."

"It doesn't have to be, Sloane."

What would she have to offer him if they continued to see each other? What if they got serious? He had his secrets and she had hers.

"Maybe it's good he's pulled away. If Johnson rehires Reed, I'll need to come home early and go into the office."

"Sloane…" Bernie remained silent for a long moment. "Is it really worth it?"

She heard the weariness in Bernie's voice, felt it in every bone of her own body. "No. It isn't. But I don't want to quit until I have another job lined up. I'll have to face it until I can find another."

"Don't come home early. Don't change your plans because of Reed. Let them do what they will. No job is worth this."

Her eyes stung. "No, it isn't."

"Fuck them," Bernie's rage and frustration came through and made her smile.

"You're right, fuck them!" She put as much feeling into it as she could.

She closed her eyes against the tears. "We'll draw unemployment together."

"That sounds good to me."

"I think I've had enough for the day." She stretched out on the couch. "Now you've talked me down, I'm going to say good night. I'll call you after I've talked to Johnson tomorrow."

"Try to rest, Sloane."

"I will." She pushed the button to end the call and threw her arm over her eyes. The silence of the condo settled in around her. She'd go on with her vacation as though Reed had never been here.

She wasn't going to wait for Connor to call either. She turned her phone off.

Fuck them both.

Men are assholes.

CHAPTER 12

CONNOR SAT IN one of the rockers on the front porch and let the soothing sound of crickets and frogs lull him back from his dark mood. He'd fucked up with Sloane. He rushed things this morning, and by pulling back tonight he probably made her feel like this morning hadn't meant anything.

She hadn't harped at him the way he deserved, or even said anything at all when he said he needed to go. What was she supposed to say when he'd been telegraphing it all the way back from the beach to her apartment? He deserved a kick in the ass. And he'd been kicking his own ass for the past hour.

He pulled out his phone for at least the twentieth time and stared at the screen. He hit Sloane's number. The call went to voice mail, and he rubbed a hand along his jaw.

"Sloane, I want to apologize for my behavior tonight. You went to an amazing amount of trouble putting the meal together, and I enjoyed every moment with you. There are things that are difficult for me to talk about... My personal life being one of them. I'd like to make up for it tomorrow if you'll give me a chance. Call me when you get this."

Why was this so hard for him? It had taken him months to talk about his divorce with Kate. After Cynthia sent him a birthday card, Kate asked him about her, and he'd given her the bare bones, but she wasn't satisfied. He'd shied away from telling her more. Because of his reticence, she read a lot of things into what he hadn't said. And things had ended between them long before he returned from his last deployment.

He turned his face away as Toby's headlights settled on him, then fell away as he turned along the drive. He'd assumed his dad would have Dorothy over, but he must have gone to her house instead. It was Connor who sat in the dark this time, not really waiting for his dad, but trying to get his act together.

Toby walked around the side of the house from the garage. "You're home early."

"Yeah."

"Problem?"

Yeah. I was an asshole. "No. Sloane was tired from all the activity today."

Toby took a seat on the rocker parallel to his. "If she doesn't swim much, that's understandable."

"She's actually a pretty good swimmer, and she picked up the basics of how to use all the equipment as easily as some of our BUD/S guys. She even spent some time in the pool today doing some underwater meditation."

"Underwater meditation huh? Is that a new technique taught on Coronado now?"

"No. She says being underwater is a little claustrophobic for her and the exercises helped her relax and control her breathing."

"You may not want to push her, Connor."

"I'm not. I told her today she doesn't have to go through with a dive unless she really wants to. I'm leaving it up to her. If she decides to give it a try, we'll need you to spot us sometime next week. I think we should do a thirty-minute shallow dive."

"Let me know at least a day in advance and I'll do it."

"Thanks."

"Four months isn't that long," Toby said. "You can keep in touch with her until you're out."

"Are you matchmaking, Dad?"

"Maybe a little. I *really* like her, and she can *really* cook."

He thought of that little carrot flower and flinched. "She enjoys it too." He stood up. "I'm going to go for a drive, Dad."

Toby drew a deep breath. "What's eating at you, Connor?"

It was time he owned up. "I was a lousy husband to Cynthia, Dad. An even lousier boyfriend to Kate. Because I can't share most of what I do, I'm even worse about sharing other things. It's—It feels like I'm ripping skin off just getting the words out.

"Sloane wasn't tired. I managed to let things from the past get in the way between us. Things that are easy to put aside when I'm on the job. I can keep my focus on what I need to do, throw the other stuff in the footlocker and shut the lid, but when the mission's over, and every moment of my day isn't spoken for… It's the reason Cynthia and I divorced, and it's the reason Kate moved out. It's the reason I'm leery of leaving the teams. If I don't have something to distract me, I'll actually have to think about everything that happened."

"Maybe you need to see someone, Connor?"

The quiet concern in his father's voice only intensified the guilt. He drank his way through his grief before, and now it had come back to haunt him. Once he started pouring it all out, all the pain would eat him up. "She'd be nine next week, Dad."

"I know." There was a hitch in his father's voice.

The pain rose up like an open wound inside him. He walked down the steps and around the house to the car. He wanted a drink. He wanted to drink until he couldn't think anymore. But he'd learned it didn't solve anything. He'd just wake up tomorrow with a splitting headache, and the grief would still be there.

He needed…he needed something. He just didn't know what could ease this. For five years he'd been running away from it by putting his time into the job. Until the little girl in El Salvador broke open the wound and left it weeping.

The forty-minute drive leveled him out some. The clock on the radio read a few minutes after eleven when he parked, walked up the steps, and rang the doorbell.

After a few minutes, the door cracked as far as the metal security guard would allow it to and Sloane peered out. "Connor?"

"I know it's late, but I don't want to wait until tomorrow to apologize to you for leaving the way I did."

He hadn't thought through what he was going to say, and for a moment his brain shut down. If he didn't start opening up to someone he….

"The little girl we saw on the beach…" The pain he thought he'd conquered rose up again. "I used to have this recurring dream…of my daughter running on the beach, just a dark silhouette in front of me, and in the dream I know there's something dangerous just in front of her, I need to protect her. I run after her as fast as I can, but I never catch up to her." He swallowed, though his throat felt full of razors. "No matter how hard you try, there are some things you can't protect them from."

The door closed, the security guard clicked, and the door swung wide. Dressed in a lightweight gown and no shoes, Sloane stepped out on the porch. She slid her arms around him and held him tight. His arms felt wooden as he put them around her and held on. Some of his tension drained away.

"Come inside, Connor."

The lamps cast a soft glow over the living room, and there was a faint scent of garlic still lingering from the dinner they shared hours earlier. Her computer stood open on the coffee table, her slippers kicked off in front of the sofa. Sloane drew him toward the sofa and urged him to sit.

She closed the laptop. "Would you like a drink, Connor?"

"Yeah, thanks."

She went into the kitchen. Ice clinked, and a minute later Sloane came back with a glass with a finger of liquid in it.

"Thanks." He took a sip and was surprised to realize it was a rusty nail, made just the way he liked it. He cupped the glass in both hands. The lemon wedge bobbed on the surface.

"We don't have to talk unless you want to. We can just sit here together."

God, why had he walked away from her earlier? "I'm not used to talking about myself or my family. Not used to sharing."

She sat down on the couch next to him and reached for the throw on the back of the couch to spread it over her. Connor smoothed it over her knees. Sloane covered his hand with hers. "Whatever you say to me won't go any further than between us."

"I know." He took another sip of his drink. "Her birthday is next week. She'd be nine."

"Olivia?"

"Yeah." He glanced at the tattoo on his wrist.

She touched it. "I noticed it yesterday."

He nodded. "I'd been in the teams for almost a decade when we got married. I loved Cynthia, but I was still focused on the job. And then my daughter was born. And for the first time in my life there was something that meant more to me than the teams. More than anything else in the world. She was my girl." He swallowed against the ache in his chest.

"We called her Livy." He took a sip of the drink to moisten a throat gone dry. "Because she was so full of life. She ran at twelve months. Not walked, but ran. Chattered constantly. Loved music." He stared down into his glass to keep from looking at Sloane. "We had to watch her like a hawk. She was into everything. By the time she was two she could climb like a monkey and she talked. I was out of the country a lot. Talked to her on FaceTime as often as I could so she wouldn't forget me."

He closed his eyes and struggled to control the wave of emotion that threatened to overwhelm him. "By the time she was three, she was a real personality, and you never knew what was going to come out of her mouth. She loved to dance and play dress-up. Loved to be read to, and would pretend she was reading to you. She'd pick out sight words she recognized.

"One day she came home from preschool with a fever and said her head hurt. She started throwing up, and two hours later she had a seizure. Cynthia called for an ambulance. They called me in from the field, and I rushed to the hospital. It was pneumococcal meningitis. They put her in a coma because she was in so much pain." He shook his head. "She died two days later."

He drained his drink in a single gulp and set the glass on a coaster. "I used to call my mom when I got like this. But she isn't here anymore. I haven't dealt with her loss or Livy's loss very well.

Then something happened during our last deployment..." Why had that small, desperately injured child crossed his path? He'd locked away the loss of Livy in a box, all buckled down. "I can't talk about that. But it brought it all to the surface again."

He hazarded a glance in her direction to find her face wet with tears. "I'm sorry. I shouldn't have dumped all this on you."

She wiped her face with her hands and dried them on her gown, then came over and sat in his lap. Put her arms around him and held him. He crushed her close and turned his face against her shoulder. Her scent filled him. It felt as though a valve had been opened and some of the pressure released.

With her hand stroking the back of his head, massaging his neck, and her cheek pressed to his ear, the comfort she offered eased the ache.

She slipped off his lap. "Come to bed, Connor. We'll just lie close and hold each other until we can sleep." She offered her hand. "You can tell me more about her."

The way he'd left him, his dad would worry if he didn't come home. Humor finally broke through his other emotions. "I'm going to have to call my Dad and tell him I'm sleeping over."

Sloane's smile broke over into a chuckle. "How about I do that?"

CHAPTER 13

S LOANE SLIPPED FREE of the bed but paused to study Connor. He'd talked for more than an hour about Livy. And after he finally drifted off, he'd been restless, his sleep disturbed by dreams. But now his face lacked the tension of the night before. He looked younger, but not as vulnerable as he'd been last night.

She'd felt the weight of keeping the dealings of her clients private. But what she experienced couldn't come close to what rested on his shoulders and psyche when it involved the taking of lives to protect himself and others. And not being able to talk about it or share the horror of it with anyone had to be a special kind of torture.

Add to that the loss of his mother and his daughter... The pain he shared with her last night echoed inside her. He grieved for the child he lost with heart-crushing intensity, and she grieved for the one she'd never have.

Though he wrapped his arms around her in his sleep, she'd held him and soothed him when the dreams came.

She crept out of the room and went downstairs to make coffee. She'd promised Bernie she wouldn't worry about things at the office, and there was nothing she could do to change things. But she wanted a heads-up at least.

With her attention focused on Connor last night, she'd been able to set it all aside, but now dread brought a tremor to her hands, and her stomach knotted.

She poured a cup of coffee and took it and her cell out on the small balcony to sit and coax herself into the right frame of mind to deal with this next hurdle.

Setting aside the cup, she did her breathing exercises to release what anxiety she could. The fragrance from the shrubs Toby gave her the day before seemed to soothe her.

She would remain professional no matter what happened, no matter what was said. She needed to put this behind her.

She dialed the office number, and, recognizing the receptionist's voice, identified herself and asked to speak to Mr. Johnson.

"I'll transfer you to Jona, Mr. Johnson's secretary."

"Thank you."

"Mr. Johnson's office. This is Jona Mitchell speaking."

Hearing the secretary's voice gave her an idea and her anxiety eased. "Good morning, Jona. This is Sloane Bianchi."

"What can I do for you, Ms. Bianchi?"

"Has Mr. Johnson interviewed Reed Alexander to return to work?"

"He's in a meeting now with him, Ms. Bianchi."

"Will you give me a call if he offers him a contract?"

"Ms. Bianchi, I really shouldn't."

She hated to use pressure to get what she wanted from the woman. "Do you remember that zero you left off the contract for Roberts' Construction? I never mentioned the mistake to anyone, and I never would. I just want a heads-up so I can make a decision about how to proceed."

Silence hung over the line for a few seconds. "I'll call you as soon as I know something."

"Thank you, Jona. I appreciate it."

"And for what it's worth, Ms. Bianchi, we all know about what he did before, and what he tried to do. He's probably trying to do the same thing now."

She'd wondered if the office staff had picked up on what was going on. "Thank you for the warning. I'll stay on my toes, and I'll be waiting for your call."

She picked up her cold coffee and wandered back into the living room. She was refilling her cup when Connor came down the stairs, his hair tousled, his jeans zipped but not buttoned. His broad chest and torso were bare, every muscle delineated in the early morning light.

A wave of pure lust swamped her, loosening the tension from her muscles, and making her wet.

"Morning." His deep voice brushed over her taut nerves like a caress. He lifted her chin to brush a kiss over her lips. "Would you like to go out for breakfast?"

"I'm waiting for a phone call, and I'm afraid I'll miss it if I get in the shower. But after that I could be persuaded."

He eyed her questioningly. "Trouble?"

"I'm hoping not." She almost told him about Reed's visit the night before, but held it back. He'd be upset on her behalf, and there was no need. "Rumor has it that my ex may be returning to the firm. I should know shortly if it's true."

"And if it is?"

"I'll have to resign. I won't work with him. But I'll try to negotiate a severance package for leaving quietly."

"And Bernie?"

"For her, too. And if that doesn't work, we'll both apply for unemployment. She and I talked last night and decided the job just isn't worth it. The working conditions we've both endured this year…" She shook her head. She wouldn't whine to him about it. It was nothing compared to what he'd endured. She lay awake half the night thinking about that.

"I'm sorry, Sloane."

Her composure wavered, and she bit her lip. "I'm going to try to look at this as an opportunity, and the impetus to move on to better things."

"Anything I can do?"

"No. But I appreciate the offer. I have coffee made if you'd like some."

"I would."

After handing him his coffee, she sat down on the couch to

keep from pacing. When the phone rang, she reached for it. "Hello."

"This is Jona. He's offering him the standard contract. The salary isn't as high as yours, but then he only worked here two years before."

She'd been with the firm six years. She'd thought she might one day make partner. "Thanks for letting me know."

"What do you plan to do?"

"I don't know. I have to think it through."

"I'm sorry, Ms. Bianchi."

Jona's sympathy caught her off guard, and her eyes stung with quick tears. "Thanks, Jona. I'll be okay. I still have some time."

When she hung up, Connor sat down next to her.

"You could go in and just say, 'Fuck it. He's not running me off.'"

"I can't work with him, Connor. He hates my guts for costing him his job. How weird is that? There's a sense of controlled violence about him when he's anywhere near me now, and I know it wouldn't take much for it to tip over into the real thing.

"He was never that way before. Reed can be very charming when he wants to be, but he's also very selfish. I knew that, I just didn't realize how selfish. He really believes he's entitled to my job. But the truth is he's a mediocre attorney. And by taking him back in the fold, Johnson is leaving his company open to problems. But if I tell him that, he'll believe it's sour grapes because of our ended relationship."

"That will be his problem now, Sloane."

"Yeah, it will."

"It sounds to me like this Reed guy may be on the edge. Does he have money problems?"

She wouldn't tell him how stupid she'd been. "He had loans he was paying off when we were together. I don't know about now. That will be Johnson's problem, too." It was almost a relief not to have a choice.

"What do you plan to do?"

"I'll take some time after I get back from vacation, probably a month, to switch things over to the other lawyers in the firm. I'll want to personally pick and choose who my clients go to."

"Can you do that?"

"Yeah, I can. But I'll have to do it discreetly."

"That way Reed won't get any of them."

"Exactly. Let him start from scratch and bring in his own clients."

"I'd have never guessed you'd be so sneaky."

She smiled. "I can be when it's called for."

"I like that."

She laughed and rose. "I'm going to go take a shower and get dressed."

"Can I come, too?"

She grinned. "As long as you don't hog all the water."

She decided sharing a shower with Connor was the best release from worry and stress she'd ever experienced. His big, strong, sensitive hands working their magic over her wet, soapy back, her shoulders, her breasts, coaxed more than one moan from her.

Where Reed had been all about the end result, Connor enjoyed extending the pleasure. And she found touching him as exciting as having his hands on her. Running her own soapy hands over his long, lean torso, she explored the flat buds of his nipples with her fingertips while their mouths clung in long, slow, hungry kisses.

The hard length of his erection rubbed against her belly, and she cupped and stroked every inch of him, proving how perfectly male he was when he grew longer, harder.

The shower stall wasn't large enough, so after a hasty rinse they staggered out into bedroom and onto the bed. He was inside her in a second, the warm, slick heat of him nestling in her body, then moving with exquisite friction as he plunged and retreated until the pleasure was too much and she cried out, the orgasm so intense she bowed beneath him. The pulse of his release triggered an aftershock that robbed her of breath.

When her vision cleared, she focused on his face above her,

and her heart tumbled. The intimacy of last night, witnessing his pain and vulnerability, had shifted something inside her. Something she couldn't acknowledge. It was too soon.

"Don't move yet," she murmured, when he started to leave her. "I just want to feel you close to me." She'd missed a closeness she never had with Reed. But Connor was here, solid, tender, filling the emptiness and taking away the hurt.

"I forgot to use a condom, Sloane," he announced with just a hint of concern.

"I'm clean. After I found out about..." She couldn't bring herself to say his name while they were still connected so intimately. "I was tested several times."

"You don't have to worry about anything with me either."

Her eyes dropped from his face to the steady pulse in his throat. "You don't have to worry about pregnancy either. I only have a one in a million chance of getting pregnant."

A cell phone rang, a ring tone Sloane never heard before. Connor pulled away, rolled off the bed to grab up his jeans and jerked his phone free. "Evans," he answered. His intent, almost harsh expression changed his face to a stranger's. When he started talking about where he was and how many hours it would take to get back, Sloane slipped off the bed, gathered her clothes, and went into the bathroom to clean up.

He was leaving. The realization cramped her stomach and tore at her heart. She'd thought he was gone for good the night before and she was granted a reprieve. But not this time.

Feeling lost, disoriented, she dressed and brushed her teeth and hair.

GOING FROM BEING inside Sloane to dressing and leaving like this seemed completely wrong. When she came out of the bathroom, he couldn't think of a thing to say to her, so he just kept to the facts. "There's been a development and I've been called back to San Diego." He had a choice. He was on leave and he didn't have to return. But he'd asked to be involved in this particular takedown. He wanted it. Needed it.

But he needed Sloane, too. Something that had become evident the night before. She needed him, too.

He took two long steps, reached for her, and cupped her shoulders. "I know you haven't had any experience with what it's like to be a SEAL's girlfriend. When I'm called up, I have to go, Sloane."

She nodded, and for a moment he thought she might cry, but she held it together—which made him proud of her at the same time his lungs tightened.

Her throat worked as she swallowed. "I understand."

"Thank you for last night, Sloane. I really needed someone to hold on to."

"I did you, too."

Her response gave him pause. "Once we're wheels up, I may be in a place where I can't get a call out. I won't know until I get there. But as soon as I'm able to, I'll call you."

She nodded. She cleared her throat. "Do you need me to drive you to the airport?"

"Yeah, that would be good. I'm flying out of Savannah. It's an hour's drive, and it'll save Dad from having to pick up his car in short-term parking. If it's okay, I'll leave it here, and call him to pick it up." His hands moved restlessly, smoothing her hair, gripping her hands.

"You're not going back to get your things?"

"No, there isn't time. The earliest flight I could get leaves in two hours."

He gripped her hands hard. "When I get back, we'll finish our challenge, Sloane. I want more time with you."

"Okay."

"This will be my last deployment. I've signed the paperwork and it's ready to go in the mail. I'll get Dad to send it for me."

But it might be weeks—it could be months. He still belonged to Uncle Sam for four more months. And she'd go on with her life. Anything could happen.

But this mission might help him finish something that had haunted him for months. And he'd be able to leave the teams with nothing left undone.

He wasn't throwing away something special. He planned to come back to something new he'd just started. "We're not ending anything. We're just postponing things for a little while. I hope you'll wait for me."

CHAPTER 14

CHARLESTON, SOUTH CAROLINA
4 Weeks later

SLOANE SCANNED THE café as she waited for Amy Schumer. The place was only open part of the day, and stayed busy from opening to closing. The large windows let in the midsummer sun while a wall of greenery brought the outdoors into the space. Though they had outdoor seating, she'd opted for a corner table for two so she and Amy would have some privacy.

When she saw her enter the café, she stood so Amy wouldn't have to look for her. As Amy walked toward her, Sloane was struck by her tall, elegant figure. Reed wasn't really consistent with any type. The secretary was short and plump, the intern thin and delicate. Amy was as big a departure from Sloane's own coloring and curves as the others.

"Thanks for joining me," she said as Amy reached her.

Amy swept a gorgeous fall of blond hair back over her shoulder. "I don't really want to trade war stories about Reed."

"That's not why I called you."

"Then what is it?"

"He's returned to Hadley, Childers, and Johnson."

"I'm sorry. I know how uncomfortable that must be for you."

"Not nearly as uncomfortable as I want to make it for him. I want to take him down. No one at your father's firm can talk to me, so I'm hoping you're still mad enough to dish some dirt on him to help me do that."

Amy's smile was gleeful. "I'd love to do that. And I might just know a few people at the office who might talk to you off the record as well."

It seemed Reed had a habit of making enemies wherever he went, along with his inability to remain faithful. "Please have a seat."

Forty-five minutes later, when she left the café, she felt more hopeful than she had since returning from vacation. Amy was more forthcoming than she'd expected, and even promised to have a couple of friends call Sloane later.

When her phone rang, she thought it might be her office calling, but the number was odd. It had a country code at the beginning. "Hello?"

"Sloane?"

She had never believed that a heart could leap, but hers did. "Connor. Are you okay?" She moved farther away from the restaurant, toward her car, so she could hear better.

"I'm good. How are you doing now you're back to work?"

"It's been busy and awkward. Reed is back. He moved back into his office before I got back from vacation."

"How's that going?"

"I haven't spoken to him. I'm keeping my distance and so is he."

"Hang tough, you've got this."

Her eyes stung at his support. "Are you eating okay and staying safe?"

"Yeah. It's hot, muggy and buggy. You'd be bathing in bug repellent. I am most of the time."

He was somewhere south. Was it buggy in the desert? "Do you know how long you'll be? Forget I asked that. I know you can't tell me."

"No, I can't, honey. I know I don't have any right to ask you to wait for me. We only had five days together."

"Almost six. You owe me a dive and a jazz concert, so I'm

going to hold you to those as soon as you get back."

He fell silent for a moment. "You've got it, I promise. How's Bernie?"

"She's good. All the bruising is gone, and she got two weeks of being waited on hand and foot out of it."

He chuckled.

"Have you talked to your father?"

"No, this is the first time I've gotten access to the phone, and I'm hoping you'll be willing to call him for me."

"Of course. He called me after you left just to reassure me you'd be okay."

"I'm glad. He mailed the last of the paperwork for me, Sloane. This will be my last deployment."

"It will go by fast." *Oh God, don't let anything happen to him, this close to getting out.* "We'll go out and celebrate as soon as you get back."

"It's a date. You haven't interviewed for another job yet, have you?" he asked.

"No. Not yet. I decided to look into some things first."

"Meaning?"

"Background dirt on Reed. He's too good, too polished at what he does. I think he's pulled this crap before, so I'm looking into some recent developments."

"Be careful, Sloane. When you stand between an asshole and what he thinks he deserves, there could be some kickback." Static nearly drowned out his last word, then cleared.

"I'll be careful." Her throat ached with tears she tried to suppress. "I wish I hadn't wasted so much time before we made love. I wanted to that first night."

"I did too. I guess it was pretty obvious."

She laughed. "Yes. We'll make up for lost time when you're home."

"Now I won't be able to think of anything else."

There was noise on the other end of the phone. Sharp, loud noises that had her heart lunging into her throat.

"I have to go."

Tears streamed down her face. "Are you okay?"

"It's just the guys coming in from the field. No worries."

"Okay." Legs weak with relief, she leaned back against her car. "Call me whenever you can," she managed.

"I will, Sloane."

The phone went dead.

CONNOR'S THOUGHTS DRIFTED to Sloane for the hundredth time in the two hours since he took over surveillance from blue team. He'd been replaying their conversation She'd sounded good. Strong. The best thing was she still wanted to see him when he got back. Surprising after four weeks of no contact.

He was still shocked that he'd opened up to her. He was torn between embarrassment and relief when he thought about it. The way she wrapped herself around him. God, he needed to get her out of his head and concentrate on the front door through the scope.

He was sick of waiting for Diaz. He wanted the drug kingpin responsible for the murder of numerous people in the region to show himself. Cowering in the stronghold the man called a house, he rarely left it without an army for protection.

The only place he went was his mistress's house. The mistress lived next door to a family who had been unlucky enough to get in the way of Diaz and his men during a visit. A stray bullet fired by the fucker at her father injured and killed the little girl, and she bled to death before they could do anything for her.

That was months ago, and the fucker was still breathing. Still wreaking havoc on the innocent people around him—him, his drug distribution network, and his thugs, who'd as soon kill a child as look at her. Just like their boss.

Connor had dealt with injured and dying kids before, but something about the little girl, the look in her eyes as she bled to death, stuck with him. She had dark eyes like his Livy. Was the same age. It didn't take a headshrinker to figure out why it bothered him so much. Hell, it had gotten all the men up in arms.

But now he had the El Salvadorian and American governments' permission to take the fucking monster down. He just had to catch him waving a gun around, threatening someone, and he could do it.

But that was the trick. He had to prove an imminent threat to someone before he could pull the trigger. They'd been watching all afternoon, hoping to catch some kind of action going down, while another sniper team was set up across town, waiting at another location, hoping for the same thing when Diaz returned from his visit to his mistress.

El Salvador, Ecuador, and Honduras were the three countries in an area known as the western triangle, the most violent areas in South America. All three territories were run by drug kingpins, their distributors and gangs.

Every nineteen hours a woman was killed in El Salvador by gang members. It was a common gang initiation ritual to rape and murder women of all ages. Gangs were the reason behind the hundreds of women fleeing the country to seek asylum in America. Gangs born in the United States had migrated south, where they could prey on a less-protected population.

The rise of Carlos Diaz had finally sent alarm bells off with the El Salvadoran government. And they had reached out for help. If Connor's team could take out Diaz and some of his henchmen, the Salvadorian government and its army might gain better control of the region, and help prevent the drugs from reaching the U.S.

Seaman D. B. Sutton, the FNG—Fucking New Guy—on the team, was acting as his spotter. He had completed his training as a sniper, but needed more experience in the field, so they were paired. The FNG was doing okay aside from eating more than any three guys and not gaining a pound. Even as he thought it, D. B. said, "Hungry, yet, Hammer?"

Connor never wavered his attention from the scope he watched through. At least he was more comfortable here than he'd been in many other environments. He had a sleeping bag to cushion his position atop the table, a bathroom, and with so many other windows in the area, no one would pinpoint where the shot had come through fast enough to shoot back.

"No, not hungry yet, but you can go ahead and feed your tapeworm." He couldn't see D. B.'s smile, but he sensed it.

"He can wait awhile yet."

The door to the house they were survielling opened. "We have movement."

D.B. jerked his binoculars up and focused in on the house.

Diaz emerged, his hand locked around the wrist of a woman—his mistress, Yessenia. She'd been roughed up, her face bloody. Though she fought against him, he dragged her out of the house, across the stoop, and down the stairs.

"Three kids are in the doorway, but they're staying put," D.B. said.

Diaz beckoned to one of his men, and the guy rushed up. He removed a gun from beneath his jacket and handed it butt-first to his boss. Diaz pulled the trigger and shot the man in the chest three times.

"I'm taking the shot," Connor focused in on Diaz's body mass, released his breath and pulled the trigger.

Blood blossomed on Diaz's white shirt, and he dropped. The woman leapt to her feet, ran back into the house, and slammed the door.

For a minute chaos reigned. The protection detail in Diaz's party stayed hunkered down behind vehicles, waiting for more gunfire.

"We need to bug out. Once they calm down they'll start looking through every building, and they'll have an army to do it." The neighbors hadn't seen them come in, but chances were they heard the shot and would recognize where it came from.

While Connor unhooked the tripod from the sniper rifle and stuffed it in his pack, D.B. reported back to their base.

"Extraction team will meet us three blocks west and pick us up." D.B. reached for his pack and his MP-5 machine gun.

After tossing the sleeping bag into the closet, Connor scanned the room for any further evidence of their occupancy. The table and two chairs sat in the middle of the room atop a rug, worn threadbare in spots and stained black in others.

The dirt and dust on the floor had been disturbed, but nothing else.

Connor slung the rifle on his left arm, drew his sidearm, and cracked the door. Finding the hall empty, he slipped out. D.B. followed.

Their boots on the stairs sounded too loud as they double-timed it down and out the back door. The sun was setting when they cut down the narrow alley that ran behind the buildings, leapfrogging from one obstacle and shadow to the next.

A long row of apartments and stores was attached, and Connor felt a nervous rush of claustrophobia. They were trapped between the buildings like fish in a barrel. At the first narrow alley leading out of the corridor, he darted through it to the main street, where he holstered his weapon, then pulled the dark blue baseball cap from his jacket pocket and put it on.

They reached the pickup point too early. Their jeans and jackets blended in with the other people on the street, but their weapons didn't. They hung back, leaning against the side of a dilapidated apartment building with stucco peeling from it like blistered skin.

"One of us is going to have to slide out onto the street so they can see us," Connor said. "One of these people is going to call someone, and they'll be all over us."

D. B. handed off his MP-5. "I'll do it. With my coloring, I can pass for a native."

He did have the dark hair and eyes and the olive complexion of the general population. He was fluent in the language as well.

Connor hung the MP-5 over his right shoulder. D.B. walked out on the street and leaned back against the face of the apartment building. A white van slowed in front of him and the side door slid open. D. B. turned to beckon to him and drew his sidearm, his attention focused on something behind Connor.

Connor wheeled around, bringing up the MP-5. As the first bullet hit him high in the chest, he was pulling the trigger, spraying the two men with answering fire. The two went down, but so did he, the wind knocked out of him, his pack saving him from hitting his head. Encumbered by too many weapons, he rolled to his right side in an attempt to scramble up and run for the van. He got one leg under him, but the other didn't seem to want to cooperate.

More men raced toward him from the corner of the alley, and he squeezed off another round of fire, sending them dodging back behind the building.

D.B. and one of the Salvadorian soldiers working with them grabbed Connor under the arms and dragged him toward the van and inside. The door slid shut, and the van screeched off as it raced down the narrow street. They all hunkered down as bullets peppered the back of the vehicle.

D. B. jerked Connor's shirt open and pulled his vest aside. "It didn't go through."

But the bullet that hit him in the thigh had. He focused on trying to start breathing again while the Salvadorian soldier cut open his pants leg and put pressure on the wound.

Screaming pain shot up his thigh to his hip, and he glanced down to see how bad it was. He was bleeding like a stuck pig. The sight made him nauseous, so he closed his eyes.

D.B.'s voice held a note of urgency as he radioed command.

CHAPTER 15

"**H**AVE YOU HEARD from him yet?" Bernie asked, as she did every morning since Connor's last phone call three weeks before. It had been the longest seven weeks of Sloane's life. Forty-nine days of long, sleepless nights.

He called when he landed in San Diego. Called that night, after he'd "gotten his gear squared away." Called when he went wheels up the next day. That's what he called it, "wheels up." Then the call outside the café....

"No. I haven't heard from him. His father, Toby, called me. He hasn't heard from him either. He told me no news is good news."

"How can a guy just walk away and not even call his father to let him know he's okay? Are you sure this guy isn't scamming you and just stringing you along? I mean, there are computers on board ships. He could send an email."

This wasn't the first time Bernie had asked, and once again she said, "He's not where he can call, Bernie. He isn't allowed to tell me—or anyone else—where he is."

"Why is it the military is so damn...?" Bernie trailed off. "Sloane?" She lowered herself into one of the chairs in front of the desk.

Sloane tried to keep her expression under control.

"He isn't just a Chief Petty Officer in the Navy, is he?"

Sloane remained silent for a long moment, pretending to read the contract Bernie had put on her desk, stalling for a moment. She wouldn't break her promise to Connor. But she had to say something. "You know how privilege works, Bernie."

"Shit!" Bernie breathed. She stared off into space for a few seconds. "Leave it to you to find the handsomest, hunkiest guy in Hilton Head, only to have him run off to Timbuktu on some secret mission."

"He'll call me when he's back." She tried to sound as confident as she could. Though after another three weeks, it was hard to keep the faith. After all, they'd only been together five…almost six…days. But they both wanted more. She had to believe that. She *did* believe it. He'd been so tender at the airport when he kissed her goodbye. And he called her instead of his father from…Timbuktu.

"When might that be?"

"I don't know."

The phone rang, and Bernie reached for it. "Sloane Bianchi's office. This is Bernie speaking." She remained silent for a moment. "Yes, Mr. Johnson." She hung up and looked up to meet Sloane's inquiring gaze. "Mr. Johnson wants to speak to you in his office."

The two of them just looked at each other for a long moment. "He didn't say what he wants to talk to me about?"

Bernie shook her head.

"Someone at another firm may have said something to him about receiving my resume." Shit! Or he could have discovered she was arranging meetings with the other lawyers in the office in preparation for leaving. Just in case.

She didn't have anything else to lose. But if she was going to be fired, she'd unload all the dirt she'd discovered about Reed before she left. "Whatever happens, Bernie, I want you to do what's right for your family. If staying here and working with one of the other lawyers is it, do it."

"It may be nothing, Sloane."

"Maybe, but just in case—"

She realized as she walked down to the Johnson's office that she no longer felt nervous about meeting with him. It would be a relief to put it behind her.

Jona was at her desk, and smiled when Sloane came into the office. Her fireplug build, short, curly gray hair, and easy smile projected the image of grandmotherly kindness. In reality she had been Johnson's secretary for nearly twenty years and was probably tough as nails, but never acted it. "Hello, Ms. Bianchi. He's taking a call right now, but as soon as he's done, you can go in. If you'll have a seat, I'll let you know when he's off."

Sloane took a seat in one of the large leather chairs.

"Can I get you anything?" Jona asked.

"No, I'm fine."

"How was your vacation?"

Sloane's smile felt bittersweet. "It was good. I learned how to scuba dive." Her eyes stung, and she blinked. Connor had been so patient, with a sense of humor. It was then she'd realized what kind of SEAL he was. How could he walk away from that?

If something happened to him...it would be the biggest regret of her life if they didn't get to finish what they started.

"That sounds scary." Jona's comment brought her back to the present.

"It was a little, but my instructor was top-notch, and I felt safe with him."

"I bet that helped."

"Yes, it did. I've decided that I'm going to try something I haven't ever done before every month from now on."

Jona dropped her chin to look over her glasses. "That doesn't mean you're going to go bungee jumping off skyscrapers or anything, does it?"

"I don't think bungee jumping will be on my list. But skydiving might." Connor would have parachuted out of planes in his job.

Jona gave a shudder. "Maybe just a helicopter ride instead." She glanced at the phone. "Mr. Johnson is off now." She pressed a button on the base, lifted the receiver, and told Johnson that

Sloane was waiting. "You can go right in, Ms. Bianchi."

"Thanks, Jona."

Sloane wiped her sweaty hands on the sides of her skirt as she approached the door, tapped it, then opened it and walked in.

Clay Johnson rose from behind his desk and stepped around it to greet her. Though in his late fifties, his silver gray hair was thick, and his build lean and athletic. She'd been told he played golf and tennis each once a week. "How are you, Sloane?"

"I'm fine, sir." She scanned Johnson's expression in an attempt to read his mood.

"Please have a seat."

She smoothed her skirt over her knees, though her attention remained on him.

"I wanted to call you in and personally tell you how impressed I've been with your work. Especially on the Olson case."

"Thank you, sir."

"You're a valued member of our firm, Sloane."

"Thank you."

"I realize how uncomfortable it must be for you for Reed to return to work here."

Then why did you hire him back?

When she didn't comment, he moved on.

"You've behaved with a great deal of professionalism, and we appreciate it."

She remained silent.

"I have a very big favor to ask of you."

"Yes sir?"

"I'd like you to bring Reed on as backup counsel for some of your newer clients. At the moment he hasn't very many, and it will free you up to give your more established clients more attention."

She'd known this moment would come. Prayed it wouldn't, but knew it would. "I can't in good conscience do that, sir."

"I know you and Reed had a tumultuous end to your relationship."

"It has nothing to do with our ended relationship, sir."

His eyes narrowed. "What does it have to do with, then?"

"When Reed was here before, and while I worked seventy-hour weeks to ensure I built my client list, he didn't bring in his own clients, sir. He depended on the overflow for his income."

"He lived with me for two years. And spent more time out on the golf course or playing poker, shoring up his relationship with your son, than he did networking or pursuing his career. What that tells me, sir, is that he's lazy.

"If you had a daughter, sir, he'd have chosen a very different route to success, as he attempted to do with his last position at Hunt, Franklin, and Schumer. Which ultimately went south when Mr. Franklin's daughter caught him in their pool house with another woman during a party."

"How did you find out about that?"

"I spoke with two people very close to the situation That aside, sir, he wasn't released from his contract with their firm because of the indiscretion in the pool house, but for ethics violations, because he slept with a client and then tried to pressure her into changing her accounts from another attorney. He threatened to tell her husband if she didn't. She marched in and told the bosses about it."

"When did you hear about this?"

"When I returned from vacation. I worked from what was said, and traced a pattern of behavior to several other people with whom he's used similar methods. He's a con man, sir. All charm and smiles and out for an easy way into billable hours."

His silence stretched, though his expression remained neutral. She decided she wouldn't sit down at a card table with him for the world.

"Everything you've told me…do you have proof, or is it all rumor?"

"I trust the sources who gave me the information." She balled her hands into fists to still their shaking. "You can call it all rumor, but with the firm's reputation at stake, if there's any truth there…it would be worth making certain, wouldn't it, sir?

When Johnson remained silent, she said, "But until I'm sure of his…trustworthiness…I really don't feel comfortable having

Mr. Alexander work with my clients. It's my duty to protect their interests. Placing them with someone I don't trust… I couldn't do that in good conscience, sir."

He brushed his already perfect hair back with a distracted gesture. "I appreciate you bringing your concerns to my attention, Sloane."

When his silence stretched again, she said, "Perhaps you can allow Mr. Alexander the opportunity to work with you, sir. You mentored me so well on the Olson trial this past year, I'm sure he could benefit from the same attention, and you could observe the quality of his work."

"I see your point. Perhaps he would." The blandness of his expression was almost frightening. "I think that will be all, Sloane."

"Thank you, sir."

Relieved to have the conversation over, she rushed to leave, then hesitated at the door. Spoke without turning to look at him. "Mr. Johnson…if there's an issue here I'm unaware of…you have the weight of the entire firm behind you, sir."

She wasted no time in exiting his office, and was trembling as she hurried down the hall toward her own. As she passed Reed's office, he stepped to the door and called her name.

She would have kept going, but out of concern that he might follow her and cause a stir in front of other clients, she stopped and half turned, but didn't look at him.

"I hope you're going to be professional about our working together, Sloane."

"I have been professional. I've stayed the hell away from you, and I'd suggest you do the same with me."

His phone rang, and he darted to his desk to answer it.

Sloane beat a path to her own office, beckoning to Bernie as she passed her.

Bernie's eyes were sharp, searching, as she entered the inner office and shut the door.

"Johnson was going to put him in charge of my newest clients and force me to work with him."

"But you changed his mind."

"For the time being." She took a deep breath to try and calm herself. "I didn't let him know I've introduced them all to some of the other attorneys in the office and already paired them up to take over, should I have to leave."

"And you dished the dirt?"

"He was so quiet. I think he was stunned. I laid it on thick about how I've brought most of my clients into the firm myself and they deserve the highest level of service we could give them. I planted the seed about Reed's ethics violations, and how he might want to dig around some himself. Then I suggested Reed could be a better attorney if he mentored him as he had me."

Bernie burst out laughing. "Oh my God! That was perfect. Inspired, even."

"It may stand up, or it may not."

"What will you do if it doesn't, Sloane?"

"I can't work with Reed, Bernie. I don't trust him. He'll find a way to destroy my reputation, steal my clients, or bill them more than they should have to pay. I'll send out a letter warning all of them to stay clear of him if he forces my hand. And I'll find a way to take him down."

Anger tightened her jaw. "He's a con artist. He took me for more than my affection. He used me. I supported him for nearly two years while he paid next to nothing in expenses. He said he had loans to pay off. But he always seemed to have money for drinks with the guys or their poker night.

"The only smart thing I did was not loan him money. And he was smart enough not to ask. I won't let him fleece our clients." She glanced away as reaction set in and she began to tear up.

And his last and lowest blow was using her inability to have children as his excuse for dumping her. And she was grateful, because by doing that he'd truly killed any feeling she had for him.

Bernie hugged her, and she clung for a moment.

"Why don't I screen your calls for a few minutes so you can sit quietly and shake this off. You've gotten the worst of it behind you. Also, you have twenty minutes before your appointment with

Mrs. Sawyer."

Sloane settled at her desk and took deep, relaxing breaths. Bernie was right. She needed to pull it together.

She longed to hear Connor's voice, to talk to him, and be nourished by the confidence he projected.

To know he was okay. The unknown was wreaking havoc with her nerves.

She needed to feel him next to her in bed, to have his arms around her.

And she might never have that. For all his promises, he might come home and not even call. Or he might not make it home. If that happened…

Would Toby call and let her know? Surely he would.

All those things weighed on her at night, when she was alone. Not knowing if he was okay was the worst.

She had to put all this aside and face her next client. Nausea rolled over her, she broke out in a cold sweat, and she rushed to the bathroom. The soup she'd eaten for lunch came up in a rush, and she heaved for several more minutes until there was nothing left.

She shivered as she pushed to her feet and rinsed her mouth. Tearing off a strip of paper towels from the dispenser, she folded and wet them, pressing the pad to the back of her neck while she fished in the bag she kept in the vanity for a toothbrush and toothpaste.

By the time Mrs. Sawyer showed up, whatever made her ill had passed, and she was able to greet her with a semblance of professional decorum.

She'd never order soup from that restaurant again.

CHAPTER 16

CONNOR WAITED FOR the aircraft to empty before levering himself out his seat. The flight attendant brought him his crutches with a smile. Blond, slender, with sculpted cheekbones and pale green eyes, she was a stunner.

"I know I shouldn't say this, but I have about four hours before I fly out."

He studied her almost perfect features and realized her very white and attractive smile didn't do a thing for him. He was looking for gold-toned brown eyes and a lush mouth he couldn't seem to get enough of, or stop dreaming about. "If I weren't already taken, I'd be thrilled to take you out to dinner. But I owe my lady a jazz concert, a diving lesson, and about six weeks of phone calls and dinner dates."

The disappointment in her expression flared into a rueful smile. "She's a lucky lady."

"I'm a lucky guy." Or at least he hoped he'd get lucky…if Sloane forgave him for not calling in the past three weeks. One call in seven weeks did not a romance make.

He slid his backpack on and reached for his crutches. He'd been on them for about a week, and had to wait until he'd gotten his stitches out before traveling. But he wasn't supposed to walk miles through airports on his leg yet.

"If you ask any of the airport employees who work the desks, they can call for a cart to pick you up and take you to get your luggage."

"Thanks." He looked at her nametag. "Heather."

"You're welcome. Have a good time in Charleston."

"I hope to."

After doing as she suggested, he took a taxi to the hotel, though it cost a small fortune. He dumped his bags in the room, then pulled his cell phone free of his backpack, called Hadley, Childers, and Johnson, and asked for Bernie.

Her voice came across the line, her New York accent triggering a smile. "Bernie, this is Connor Evans."

"Oh my God, what are you doing calling me?"

"I wanted to come to the office, but don't want to interrupt Sloane while she's working."

"You're here in Charleston?"

"Yes. I just flew in about half an hour ago."

"Her last appointment for the day is already here, and she'll be through in a few minutes. Sloane doesn't usually leave until five thirty or six. Is this supposed to be a surprise?"

"Yes. She doesn't have plans for dinner, does she?"

"No."

"What's her favorite food besides Italian?"

"Actually there isn't any kind of food she doesn't like. She loves fish. There's Hank's fish house. And she loves Magnolias. They serve a little of everything, and it's all excellent. My husband took me there for our anniversary. It's that kind of place."

"I'll call and try to get reservations there. Thanks, Bernie. How is she?"

"A little stressed, but dealing with it. She's lost a little weight. I think she's pining for you."

"She doesn't need to lose any weight. Her curves are just right."

"Awww. I'll tell her you said that after the surprise. Now get your ass over here."

He laughed. "I'm on my way."

He called downstairs to order a taxi, then dealt with making the Magnolias reservation.

He couldn't get across town fast enough, but a thought occurred to him, and he tapped the window between them. "I need to make a stop. I want to get something for my lady. Any suggestions?"

After a quick discussion and an equally quick stop, he set his pack gingerly between his feet so the he wouldn't crush the flowers. With both hands committed to the crutches, it was the only way he could carry things.

Her office building was lodged between a shop on one side and another office on the other. The façade gleamed white, while black shutters framed each side of the large windows, and the front door was painted a dark crimson. When he entered the lobby a receptionist looked up.

"You must be Chief Evans. Bernie described you perfectly. She told me to direct you to the second floor, first office on the right. There's an elevator just down the hall on the left. Do you need any help?"

"No, thanks. I'm fine."

Once he was riding the elevator, his heart raced, and he admitted to being a little nervous. If she was pissed at him, he could talk her down. If she'd lost patience and moved on in the last four weeks, he'd do his damnedest to win her back. He rested his weight on the crutches long enough to rake his fingers through his hair. He should have gotten a haircut. He was looking shaggy and it curled around his ears.

Bernie sat in a chair in the reception area. Her face fell when she saw his crutches. "I don't suppose you'll tell me what happened?"

He started to say he'd slipped in the shower, but her open concern killed that idea. "Some bad guys picked on me."

Her lips twitched at his whiny tone. "I hope you kicked their ass."

"You could say that."

"Good." Her satisfied look triggered a smile. "Come this way."

He swung forward.

"How long are you going to be on the crutches?"

"Another two weeks—whenever I go out, at least. I can walk around at home as long as I don't overdo it."

"Bummer."

He chuckled at her heartfelt, succinct sympathy as she led him into a sort of outer office that seemed to be her space. Pictures of a man, her sister, and two children were displayed on a floating shelving unit behind the walnut desk.

"She's had an eventful day. I hope you'll be the cherry on top to make it all right."

"I'll do my best."

She shot him a grin. "God, I hope you're the real deal, because if you aren't, I'm going to have to kill you." She opened the door and stepped only halfway through. "You have a visitor, Sloane."

She stepped out of the way and he swung forward.

He took in the room only as the space that surrounded her. His first thought was she looked pale, but just as beautiful as ever. Her eyes widened, and she shot to her feet, taking in his crutches even as she was hurrying toward him. Without a word she put her arms around him and held him tight. He dropped one of the crutches so he could hold her.

IT TOOK ALL her determination not to cry. "Are you okay?" It was all she could think to ask without embarrassing herself.

"Yeah. A little banged up, but I'll heal." He cupped her face in his hands and kissed her. The sweet heat rose up between them, and she leaned into him, feeling him harden for her.

"It still works," he said.

She laughed. "The kiss, or something else?"

"Both."

She bent to retrieve his crutch to hide the quick rush of tears. He could have been killed. But he wasn't. And he was home.

"I wanted to call last week, Sloane, but I was still flat on my back in the hospital, and I didn't want to worry you or Dad. I wanted to be back on my feet first."

"How long have you been back?"

"Fifteen days."

"Fifteen days," she repeated. For fifteen days she'd been lying sleepless in bed, worried he might be dying. Fifteen days she'd ached to hear his voice. Pretended he was holding her so she could sleep.

She had fallen for him. Hard. But obviously he didn't have the same feelings for her. And how could he after only five days? She'd blown everything out of proportion.

She walked back to her desk and sat down behind it. A rush of pain jumbled her thoughts with white noise, and when she looked up he was standing in front of her desk.

"I'm glad you're home safe, Connor. I worried about you." She bent to retrieve her purse from the bottom drawer of her desk. "When we met it was just supposed to be a two-week vacation thing. I thought I was up for it. And as hard as I tried to convince myself I was, I wasn't. And I'm not now."

Why was she letting herself fall into the same traps repeatedly? Stumbling into the same relationship mistakes? Letting guys play her? She'd expected too much, too soon. She'd given too much, too soon. But she couldn't go back to that carefree, live-in-the-moment, reach for what you want... She didn't even know what to call it.

She forced herself to look up at him. "You need to go see your father and let him know you're okay." She rose. "And I need to go home." Because she'd had enough for one day. She'd had seven weeks too much. And he just made it so much worse.

She rounded the desk, and he was there blocking her way. "Let me explain, Sloane."

"You don't owe me any explanations. Why would you? I was just a five-day distraction while you were on leave."

"No you weren't."

"If I wasn't, you'd have picked up the phone and called fifteen days ago." There. She'd exposed her feelings, but what did it matter? She skirted around him and rushed out of the office, her hurt bleeding over into anger.

"I'm going home, Bernie." She couldn't look at her, either. Otherwise the careful control over her emotions would snap.

"Okay." Bernie's gaze moved from one to the other. "Should I reschedule your appointments for tomorrow?"

"No. I'll be here."

"You vindictive bitch." Reed's voice was hushed, but still reached her as he advanced into Bernie's office, a box from the copy room clenched in his hands. "You just had to rock the boat. Just had to tell Johnson you wouldn't work with me."

"Did you really expect me to say I would?" Had her anger not been at its peak, she might have ignored him. "Surely you're not that obtuse."

The feral look in his eyes as he bore down on her triggered a heart-pounding rush of adrenaline, and she took a step back.

Connor swung out of her office and into Bernie's area, then staggered sideways, planting the foot of one crutch in front of Reed's shin. Reed went down and would have done a faceplant if the box he was carrying hadn't taken the brunt of his fall.

"Sorry." Connor didn't sound sorry at all. "I lost my balance."

Reed climbed to his feet and turned to glare at Connor. "Get away from me."

Connor's dark eyes went flat and cold, his body language shifting to controlled violence. He propped his crutch on the edge of Bernie's desk with slow precision. Bernie rose from her seat at the shift in Connor's expression, while Sloane took a step back from both men.

"I think you and I need to have a talk about how you address Sloane."

Rising to his full height, Reed turned to confront him, his mouth already open to speak. One look at Connor's honed features and his expression shifted to wariness, and he shut his mouth.

"You may address her as Ms. Bianchi. Sloane if she allows it.

But nothing else. That includes the term *bitch*." He bit out the word as though it tasted foul. "With two witnesses to your sexist behavior in the workplace, you could be going right back out the door before you get settled in. You might want to apologize." The implication was that otherwise he'd force him.

Reed's face was flushed, and his expression shifted between sullen and embarrassed as he looked at her. "Sorry, Sloane." He turned and beat it back out into the hall.

Sloane swallowed in an attempt to moisten her dry mouth. Connor reached for his crutches. There was nothing cold or flat in his expression as he shifted his attention to her.

Once in the elevator, Connor leaned back against the stained cherry wood interior.

"That guy's going to be trouble, Sloane. Did he talk to you like that when you were together?"

"No. Never."

"He broke it off, but he's angry at you."

"So it would seem."

Connor shook his head. He reached for the button that stopped the elevator. Sloane looked up in surprise. "What I need to say, I need to say in private. Eighteen days ago, I had to have emergency surgery to repair a bullet wound to my thigh. Three days later I was flown to San Diego and taken to Balboa Military Hospital. I had an infection, and I was told I might lose my leg."

His words felt like a punch, and she tried to swallow but couldn't.

"The docs had to open up the wound and let it drain. Luckily the artery they grafted in to replace the one damaged by the bullet was still okay. It was touch and go for about a week, and I'll have a hell of a scar, but it's mending." He shook his head. "I could make the excuse that I was in no shape to call, but I won't, because I could have. But I just didn't think it would be fair to drop that on you, Sloane."

"And if you'd lost your leg?" she asked, feeling sick because he'd been so badly hurt. That his leg would be forever marred by violence she only understood peripherally.

"I don't know."

"You'd never have called me again. You'd have gone on with-out letting me know what happened, or if you did call, you'd have broken things off without telling me anything about what hap-pened."

"I don't know what I would have done. I just couldn't see myself calling you and dropping all of *this,*" he motioned at his leg, "on you."

Her chest ached with tears. "Do I seem like a shallow person to you, Connor?"

"No."

"Then why would you treat me like I am?"

He ran his hand back and forth over the top of his head, roughing up his hair. "What would you have done if I'd called and told you about my leg?"

"Whatever you needed me to do." She pushed the button, the elevator descended, and the door opened. She stalked out and turned left toward the back door.

"Sloane."

She turned to face him, trying to keep her expression as in-tractable as possible. But she wanted to cry. For them both. Because he was so locked-down emotionally, so afraid of getting hurt he wouldn't let anyone in. But he had that last night in Hilton Head. And obviously she read too much into it.

"As soon as they said I could travel, I came here. I have din-ner reservations at Magnolias at seven. And I have a bouquet in my backpack that's probably wilting as we speak. I have seven weeks of things I wanted to say to you while I was gone, and couldn't because I didn't have access to a phone."

Damn him. She didn't want to hear this.

She needed to cut her losses.

She stared at the floor for several seconds, because to look at him would rob her of her composure. "Where are you staying?" She needed her head examined.

"The Vendue."

She was surprised.

"I thought you might like it."

Damnit, he's too smart for his own good. He made it hard to stay angry. But the hurt was still there. "My car is this way."

She pushed the passenger seat all the way back for him, and took his backpack so he could get in the car. Once he was settled, she set his pack between his feet and loaded his crutches into the back seat. "You need to get off that leg and elevate it." Even through his dark pants she could see the swelling. She closed the door.

Once she was in the driver's seat, she said, "I appreciate the reservations at Magnolias, but I ate some soup at lunch that disagreed with me, and I'm still a little out of sorts. I probably need to stick with something light for dinner and see how I do."

"Okay. I'll cancel and make it for another night if you like."

For the first time she heard a little uncertainty in his voice.

"Why is it so hard for you to turn to anyone for help, Connor? You look to your team for help, don't you?"

"Not for this. To do what we do, we have to maintain the idea that we're indestructible. We can't think any other way. To bring them into this would be like asking them to face what could be possible for them all. We don't give up, Sloane. Never. I was down, bleeding, but I was still firing, covering the guys carrying me to transport."

But he was willing to walk away from her. "Maybe you need to carry some of that attitude over into your personal life."

When his lips tightened, she knew she'd hit a nerve.

CHAPTER 17

S HE WAS CERTAINLY in the right profession. She went right for the weak spot. He wouldn't say the jugular, because she wasn't bloodthirsty enough for that.

By trying to protect her, he'd hurt her. Badly. She'd have flown out to San Diego. She'd have done whatever he asked of her. And now he felt like an asshole again. But he also felt hope.

She reached for the keys and started the car. They drove in silence until they reached her apartment building. It was smaller than he had envisioned, only four stories tall, but the balconies were large enough to hold a grill and a table and chairs.

Sloane lived on the third floor. Thank God for elevators.

She unlocked her apartment and stood back to allow him to enter first.

"A year and a half ago I moved from my apartment downtown to here. The rent on the other place was expensive and, being alone, I didn't need all that space. At the time I thought I might end up being fired because of the lawsuit, so I needed to get my expenses down as much as possible. I'm saving for my house with the extra.

"There's a pool around back and a exercise room, but I'm usually too busy to use either."

"This looks about the same size as mine."

He propped his crutches by the door and paused to take everything in. There were photos of her large Italian family on an entrance table. And above them hung a watercolor of a plantation house under moss-draped trees in bold shades of blue, red, and green.

The foyer opened up into a living room that looked like a photo from a magazine. Area rugs with strong textures stretched across the floor. A large, overstuffed, dark blue couch was bracketed by end tables with brushed nickel lamps that reminded him of a woman's ripe figure. Two patterned armchairs designed like the couch created a grouping. The large, square coffee table had a top like a tray and held three large candles.

Opposite the couch a flat screen television hung on the wall, and beneath it was a waist-high bookcase filled with books, CDs, DVDs, and a unit to play both, along with several interesting pieces of art, bright watercolors of different areas of Charleston, done in a style similar to the one by the door.

Everything was tasteful and reflected her personality. The adjoining kitchen looked like her as well, with red towels, a wine rack, and small pots of herbs under a LED light.

In comparison, his looked like a place to flop for a weekend. He was glad she and his dad hadn't seen it.

"Nice place, Sloane. It suits you."

"Thank you. Why don't you have a seat and I'll get us something to drink?" He set his backpack in one of the barstools at the large island separating the kitchen and living room spaces. He unfastened the straps and took out the bouquet. Aside from one of the lilies being a little wilted, the rest were in good shape.

Sloane set two glasses of sweet tea on the island. She unfolded the paper and gently touched one of the rosebuds with the back of a finger. "This is only the third time I've been given flowers. My date for my senior prom got me an orchid wrist corsage, my parents gave me a bouquet of sunflowers when I was accepted into law school, and now you've given me my first roses."

"You've been hanging out with the wrong guys, Sloane."

She laughed, then as quickly misted up. "I shouldn't have been so angry. You were in a horrible situation with your leg and… You were right, I had no idea what being involved with a SEAL was all about."

Involved. Was that what they were? "You're the only woman I'm seeing, the only one I thought about every day I was gone. It may have only been six days, but I don't think you realize what an impression you make. It was hard as hell keeping my mind off you. I don't know where this may be going, I just know I want more."

The tension in her expression relaxed. When she nestled in against him, like she had that first night, relief stormed through him. He'd been within a gnat's ass of being kicked to the curb.

In fact, those few minutes in her office, he thought he had been. It certainly clarified his feelings for her. Finding himself on the verge of again losing something important had a way of doing that.

"After I put these in water, why don't we both take a nap? Then I'll fix something for dinner."

"Or we could go over to my hotel for dinner and wander the halls to check out the art. I only got to see a few pieces before I left to go to your office." And they would spend the night there if he could persuade her to.

"Are you trying to get me to come with you so you can show me your etchings?"

Connor laughed. "Well, officially they aren't mine. I can't even draw a stick man without the help of a computer, but yeah."

Her tawny gaze snagged on his face, and something in her expression sent blood rushing south. "After you've elevated your leg and rested from the trip, we'll talk about it. I'm going to put my roses in water."

CHAPTER 18

"HOW LONG CAN you stay?" Sloane asked while they wandered down the corridors to stop and admire the artwork displayed throughout the hotel.

He reached for her hand and laced his fingers through hers.

"I have an appointment with the doctor in two weeks, so I'll have to fly back for that. And I still have some paperwork and other things I need to take care of before I'm discharged. To relocate, I'll have to make arrangements for all my belongings to be moved. I just have the basics. A couch, a chair, a bed. Nothing fancy. I think I have more fishing and camping gear than I do furniture."

And he had the mementos of his daughter's young life that he hadn't had the courage to look at since her death. Maybe he could now.

Something had changed for him since the night he talked to Sloane about Livy. Sharing memories of his daughter that were so precious, but hard to even think about, had eased the pain. Sloane had laughed and cried and held him.

He didn't know why he'd been able to open up with her when he hadn't with Kate. Maybe it was because with Cynthia he'd been afraid of making her pain worse by sharing his. He had the idea that he had to stay strong and suppress his emotions, but in doing so had drawn further and further away from her.

"How's the leg?" Sloane asked, bringing him back from his thoughts.

"It's sore, but just walking is helping that."

"Good. But you don't need to overdo it."

They stopped to study one of the paintings done by the resident artist.

He studied the bright reds and blues. "This reminds me of the one in your entrance hall."

"The paintings at my place are my sister's work."

"That's amazing. She needs to be submitting to get her work in here."

"She has some in other galleries. I was lucky enough to buy the ones in my apartment from her while she was going to school. Now they're worth about four times what I paid for them."

"So you invested in your sister and helped her with school expenses."

"Yeah. We were raised to work hard and earn our way. But everyone needs a little help now and then."

He nodded. He glanced up and down the tiled corridor before cuddling her in close. "Will you stay the night with me here? I have a king sized canopy bed."

"What did your doctor say about carousing with women?"

"He said if it worked, I should use it."

She laughed. "I doubt that. No hanky-panky until the doctor says it's okay."

"I'll get him to send you an email."

She shook her head. "Staying at hotels here in Charleston can get expensive, Connor. You can stay with me."

He fell silent for a moment, searching her face. "I don't want to take advantage."

"I wouldn't have asked if I didn't want you there." She leaned into him when they started to walk to the next painting. "I have to go home to change for work in the morning. You can check out then."

★

LATER, WHEN THEY were lying on the bed in the room watching television, Sloane was reminded of their afternoon watching *Die Hard* and several other movies. She lay on Connor's left side to keep from touching his right thigh.

Both his legs had red scars too new to have lost their ugly color. The left was healed, the right still scabbed and bearing the evidence of the second surgery, though the stitches had been removed. The swelling she noticed earlier had subsided somewhat. But it still worried her.

She wanted to say, *don't push yourself.* But telling this man not to do something was a surefire way to get him to do the complete opposite.

"Tell me about your life in San Diego, Connor. I want to know about you."

"The guys are like a family, always watching your back..." For half an hour he shared stories of them at home, and of some things he could talk about from deployments.

When he drifted off to sleep, which proved how drained he was physically by the trip, and by his injuries and subsequent illness, she rose and took off the dark blue slacks and silk blouse she changed into for dinner, tossed her bra atop them on one of the nightstands, and put on the T-shirt Connor laid out for her.

She woke at dawn to the brush of Connor's lips against the back of her neck and a hard heat pressing against her from behind. "You can't. You need to rest your leg."

"It's not my leg that needs attention," he said, in a gravelly morning voice so sexy it lit a fuse to her own need. His fingers slid down her belly beneath her panties and found her. Her breath stuttered and she parted her legs to give him better access.

She half turned against him and his mouth found hers, his tongue mirroring what his fingers were doing. She made a sound—part plea, part moan—and she covered the hand that was giving her such pleasure as her hips rose and rolled beneath the relentless glide of his fingers against that one sweet spot, the hot heat of his erection rubbing against her hip. The orgasm rolled through her, leaving her gasping. He slowly removed his hand, leaving her aching and empty.

She stripped off her panties while he covered himself with a condom. Careful of his leg, she straddled his hips and took him in. Already sensitive from the earlier climax, she shuddered with pleasure as he filled her.

He was so swollen with need, every move she made threatened to tip her over the edge again. As she rose and lowered herself over him, she reached behind her and cupped his balls. They swelled and tightened in her hand. At the first pulse of his release, her control spindled away, and sweet pleasure found her again.

She had never known a passion like this. It was so all-consuming it was almost frightening. She leaned down to press her lips to his. The early morning sun brushed his features with soft light, and she paused just to take him in while tenderness nearly overwhelmed her. She could love him if he'd let her.

He reached up to smooth her hair back and draw her lips to his again. She scooted to the side when he slipped away to deal with the condom, then came back. When he turned to spoon in against her back and nestle her against him, she tucked his hand up beneath her cheek. He kissed the back of her neck again.

"I missed you," he murmured against her ear.

CHAPTER 19

THERE WAS NOTHING like morning sex to perk a lady up. And Connor was really good at morning sex. In fact, she was learning he enjoyed it almost as much as he did evening sex. They'd fallen into a routine of morning sex and him fixing breakfast while she showered and got ready for work.

He didn't lie about the house doing nothing. He'd been walking every day to strengthen his leg and keep the swelling down. And he worked at his computer on the drone plans, as well as doing more of the paperwork needed for his separation from the Navy. They met for lunch downtown for an hour, and then it was back to work for her.

Bernie rose and followed her into her office. "Look who's come in looking like the cat who ate the canary for the fourth day this week. You're not wearing that poor, injured man out, are you?"

"SEALs never give up. That's what Connor told me."

"Obviously even when they're injured, they rise to the occasion."

"I don't kiss and tell." She fanned her face.

"When you left here that first day, I thought you were going to send him packing."

"I was hurt. He'd been back in the country for fifteen days and didn't call. And I'd been heartsick and worried about him the whole time. Turns out his leg injury was very bad, and he had an infection. There was a chance at first that he might lose his leg. I know I was being emotional and petty, and after I calmed down, I apologized. He said he didn't call because he didn't want to dump all that on me."

"He's used to protecting his country and keeping quiet about it, Sloane. It would be his first instinct to try and protect you. Since you'd only known each other for a few days, he might have thought it was too soon to involve you in something so serious."

"I know. I know everything's moved fast."

"Your open heart is what makes people love you so easily, Sloane."

It hadn't happened with Reed. But maybe it would with Connor?

He was trying to open up to her. Trying not to hold back.

She'd even suggested inviting his father to come have dinner with them one night before Connor had to fly out. He was open to it, they just hadn't chosen the date.

She refused to look at Bernie for fear of what her friend might read in her expression. "I thought we'd knock out those letters I need to write for Sylvia Fulton first and get that off our plate."

She worked steadily for nearly three hours, until nausea crept up on her and a cold sweat broke out down the back of her neck and seemed to spread to the rest of her body. She bolted from her desk to the bathroom, the urge to heave too strong to fight. Acid burned her throat as it came up in a rush. She didn't realize Bernie was standing over her until she lifted her hair back off her neck and put a cool compress there.

After a few more unproductive heaves, the sickness began to recede. She staggered to her feet to rinse her mouth and blot the sweat from her brow.

Bernie flushed the toilet. "Is it something you ate?"

"I don't know. I was a little nauseous this morning, but it passed."

Bernie's dark brows were twisted in a worried frown. "This isn't the first time you've been sick this week, Sloane. You said the soup you ate on Monday made you sick."

"It was a little greasy."

"Tell me you haven't had unprotected sex."

"No." But she had. "Well, only once. But you know my history, Bernie. I can't be pregnant."

"That's what I said the last time, too. Even Paul kept saying it all the way to the drug store to get the test."

"The doctor said I couldn't conceive without medical intervention. My fallopian tubes are too scarred and my cycle too irregular for it to happen. It isn't unusual for me to skip periods or have painful ones."

"How long has it been since you've had a period?"

"Since a week or more before our trip to Hilton Head." Her heart pounded in her ears.

"If tab A fits into slot B and swimmers are ejected, you can be pregnant."

Sloane would have laughed had the subject not been so painful. "I do know how it works. It would be a million-to-one chance if it happened the natural way. A miracle."

She couldn't be pregnant. She wasn't. It would be finger of God stuff.

"Hey, your guy's mister super-swimmer. Maybe his swimmers are too." Bernie smiled at her and smoothed back her hair like she would one of her children. "It wouldn't hurt for you to hit a drug store to get a test. Just in case. I can go out and get one for you now, and you'll know for certain. Because of all your issues, you'll want to know right away."

Her face felt a little numb. Was she going into shock?

"I think I need to sit down."

"I think you need to lie down. You look a little white." Bernie urged her to the small couch just beneath the window. "Just rest until I get back. I'll drive down to CVS. It's the closest drugstore."

She went into the bathroom, returned with a cold compress, and laid it across Sloane's forehead. "But first I'll fix you a cup of hot tea and bring you some crackers. They should help settle your stomach."

"Thank you, Bernie."

Bernie's rushed exit left the room entirely too quiet. Disjointed thoughts tumbled through Sloane's mind. How would she handle this? How would Connor? He'd lost a child. Though it had been six years, he might not be ready to risk his heart on another. He carried around so much pain. The way he talked about his Livy... Everything was moving too fast.

Maybe it wasn't so. Maybe it was just a bug.

Bernie brought the tea and crackers, then left again with her purse over her shoulder.

Fifteen minutes later the door opened, and she turned to see who had come in without knocking.

Reed stood over her, his expression shuttered. "Hung over?"

"No. I think I have a stomach bug. If I were you, I'd keep my distance. I might throw up on you."

Uneasy with her vulnerable position, she sat up, and her stomach pitched. She placed a hand against it. Once it settled she asked, "What do you want, Reed?"

"I want your woman scorned routine to end, Sloane."

She studied him for a moment and released her breath on an exhausted sigh. "It's been a year and a half, Reed. I was hurt for a while, but then I realized you'd done me a favor by dumping me. I've moved on. I have someone else in my life. So there is no 'woman scorned routine.'" *Get over yourself, asshole.*

His jaw flexed and his hands knotted into fists. A chill rushed up her spine. This aggression from him frightened her.

Sloane reached for the cup of tea with a trembling hand and took a sip. "I think I'm feeling well enough to go back to work." She took the teacup with her in case she needed to use it as a weapon, giving him a wide berth as she moved past him and went to her desk. She felt safer with the barrier between them. But not safe enough to sit down.

"I want to be able to work with you without this coldness between us." Meaning he wanted her to share her clients with him.

She cut to the chase. "Get out and network and find your own clients."

His frustration was palpable. "You're just doing this because of what happened between us."

"I'm doing this because I have a duty to protect my clients' interests. As long as I'm physically able to serve them, I'm the only lawyer they need. Mr. Johnson worked extensively with me this past year on the trial, and I got the impression he was going to do the same with you for a while."

"Was it your idea?"

She shook her head. "Do you really think I'd have that much influence with him? Especially since I brought a lawsuit against the firm?" *Because of you.* She took another sip of the tea. "I suggest you work to expand your client base if you want him off your back. If you're busy with your own clients he won't have any reason to look over your shoulder. Send out some letters to local businesses. Pass your card out every opportunity you get."

A tap came at the door, and Bernie shoved it open, a bag in her hand. On seeing Reed, her features stiffened into a polite mask. "Can I do something for you, Mr. Alexander?"

"No." Reed turned and stalked out of the room.

"You have to tell Mr. Johnson he's harassing you, Sloane."

"This is only the second time he's spoken to me."

"There's something more there when he looks at you. He isn't right. There's a kind of desperation about him."

Bernie was right, but there was nothing she could do about Reed right now. Her thoughts focused on the bag in Bernie's hand.

Having a baby was one of her dreams. A dream she thought was forever out of her reach. It would be a gift if she was pregnant.

But if she was, it would change everything between her and Connor. He might feel trapped. He might not even believe it was his. After all, they'd been apart for seven weeks. If he walked away now, she'd never see him again. Or if he didn't, it might be only because of the baby. Having their relationship change so drastically could be devastating.

She looked up at Bernie. "Should I wait until in the morning, or should I do it now?"

"How many weeks would you be?"

"Seven almost eight."

"Do it now."

She started to tear up. "I was teasing Jona down at Johnson's office that I was going to do something I'd never done before once a month. I mentioned skydiving."

"You'll be covered for the next seven and a half months," Bernie said, her tone upbeat as she broke open the box and took out the stick. "All you have to do is pee in this cup," she held up a paper cup, "then dip in the stick. It'll take a few minutes. A plus sign means you are, a negative means you're not."

Sloane took the cup and the pregnancy test into the bathroom. Stalling, she brushed her teeth first.

As she came out, loud voices came from outside in the hall. She and Bernie moved together to the door and peered out. Two police officers were half-marching, half-dragging Reed down the hall toward the elevators.

"Keep it up, asshole, and we'll add resisting arrest to your charges."

"This is all a mistake," Reed insisted. "I'll sue you for false arrest."

Behind them Clay Johnson followed their progress while other office staff and attorneys stepped out into the hall to gawk.

"I want to call my lawyer," Reed sounded strident. With a desperate lunge, he jerked loose from one of the policemen and grabbed his gun, backhanding the other one in the face with it.

A scream came from down the hall, and people scattered. Reed pointed the gun at the cop who remained standing and backed toward Sloane's office.

"Put the gun down," the cop ordered.

Bernie jerked Sloane back, and she twisted the new lock they just installed before they rushed through her office into Sloane's and shut the door. Sloane locked that door as well. The two of them backed away and huddled near the bathroom.

A crash came from Bernie's office, and they both jerked. Bernie caught her breath.

The lock sprang like it was made out of tissue paper and the door banged against the wall.

Reed pointed the gun at Sloane. Her legs turned to water and her stomach hollowed. After seeing Connor's thigh she understood the damage a bullet could do.

"Get over on the couch, Sloane. You too, Bernie."

He shut the door, though the lock to keep it closed was useless. He dragged the small table next to it over to block it. The books on it tumbled to the floor, and he kicked them out of the way.

Sweat ran down Reed's face, and his breathing sounded ragged.

She and Bernie reached for each other and clung.

The phone started ringing. Reed jerked it off her desk and threw it against the wall. Sloane flinched at his violent reaction, and felt Bernie's shudder.

He paced back and forth like a caged animal, his large feet eating up the narrow strip of floor space in front of the desk.

"What's happening, Reed?" Sloane asked, purposely pitching her voice low.

"They're arresting me for extortion and blackmail."

She wished she was surprised, but she'd suspected he was holding something over Clay Johnson's head to get his position back.

"I'm being investigated by the state bar for ethics violations, and I was evicted from my apartment yesterday."

Three hard punches. It explained his air of desperation. "Call your lawyer, Reed. And ask him to come here."

"I don't have one. I don't have the money for one."

"Maybe Simon Stewart would take you on as a professional courtesy. He's worked with you in the past, and he used to do criminal law. Just call him. My cell phone's on the desk."

He narrowed his eyes at her. "Why are you trying to help me?"

Nausea rolled over her again, and even swallowing the saliva in her mouth made it worse. She wanted to live. She wanted to tell Connor she loved him. "Because I want to get out of here in one piece. I want all of us to do that. If the police come in here, guns blazing, none of us will."

Though he'd had the gun down by his side he jerked it up and pointed it at the door.

At least he wasn't pointing it at them.

He leaned back against her desk. "Bernie, come here."

Bernie remained where she was, her face pale with fear. "What do you want?"

"I want you to call Stewart and ask him to represent me."

CHAPTER 20

CONNOR SAVED HIS work and moved on to the next thing. Being laid up had given him a new understanding of why his mother encouraged his father to start a business. This inactivity was driving him crazy, and he'd only been out of the hospital for a few days.

He pulled up the checklist he was given by the military transition center nearly a year ago, and studied the number of things he had yet to accomplish. He'd arranged to take the last two classes of his business degree online starting in August. He was already registered, and the classes paid for.

He'd been doing some research on the jobs available close to his dad, but now he decided to research the Charleston area. A long-distance relationship with Sloane just wasn't what he wanted. Even two hours away seemed too far if they wanted their relationship to deepen.

He'd get an apartment close by. He couldn't live with her until they figured out if this thing they had would grow into something permanent. He'd work, finish those last two classes, and apply for college. Now he had a plan, he researched colleges. And realized he'd be able to go to the Citadel as retired military on the GI bill and complete a mechanical engineering degree and master's if he wanted to.

If things didn't work out for them... He wasn't going down

that road. A SEAL never gave up. Sloane was right, he needed to incorporate some SEAL attitude into his personal life.

She was too important to lose.

The thought broke his focus on the computer, and he glanced away to the balcony just outside. He was in love for the second time in his life. He loved her. Just acknowledging it helped relax some of the tension in his shoulders. But did she love him too?

She had strong feelings for him. The way she behaved when he first arrived after those fifteen days proved that. The way she responded to him in bed... He couldn't see her giving so much of herself to anyone if she didn't care deeply for them.

She'd only had three lovers before him. That told him straight up how cautious she was about who she allowed intimately close.

She loved him. She had to.

He checked his watch. He'd be early to pick her up for lunch, but he just couldn't seem to wait. He closed the computer, grabbed the keys to Sloane's car, and left the apartment.

Though he wasn't supposed to be operating a motor vehicle just yet, he seemed to be doing fine with it. It took him twenty-five minutes to get from her apartment to Radcliff Street down-town. He turned the corner, then parked in the back lot. A police car was in one of the slots. Strange.

He walked into the lobby, and the desk where the young receptionist usually sat was empty, so he moved on to the elevator. In the distance, sirens wailed.

The doors to the elevator stood open and someone had hit the lock button. Thinking something must be wrong with it, he walked over to the door just down the hall and hobbled up the steps to the second floor.

SLOANE SQUEEZED BERNIE'S hand, offering her what courage she could. Reed wouldn't hurt her as long as she was doing something for him.

The shift in his attitude toward Sloane since before coming

back to the firm was frightening. He had no reason to hurt Bernie, but Sloane could easily believe he'd be willing to take it all out on her. Sloane brushed back the lank strands of hair around her face where Bernie had rested the paper towel compress.

The nausea had finally passed, but she was feeling hollowed out from losing what little breakfast she ate this morning.

"Why couldn't you just let me work with you, Sloane?" Reed demanded. He wiped his sweating face with a Kleenex from a box on her desk.

No matter what she said it would anger him. "I trusted you once, Reed, and you betrayed me. I'm not going to let you take advantage of me again."

His rounded jaw tightened.

"You didn't really care about me at all," she added. "I realized that after the things you said when you broke it off."

"I needed money, and I knew you wouldn't loan it to me. Because of the non-compete agreement you signed here, I knew you couldn't take your clients with you, so I figured I'd get your job and clients, and I'd have cash coming in."

She was surprised she felt so little outrage at this point. She truly had moved on. "What is it? Drugs, gambling, sex?"

"Does it matter?" he bit out, his face suddenly haggard.

"No, I don't suppose it does."

Bernie interrupted them as she brought the phone to Reed. "It's Mr. Stewart." She took her place beside Sloane and dropped her voice to a whisper. "How are you feeling?"

"I'm okay. The nausea has finally passed."

"Good." She reached for Sloane's hand and tucked something into it.

It was the pregnancy test. She'd left it on the sink in the bathroom, and Bernie retrieved it while Reed was distracted.

Sloane looked down at it, then tucked it into her bra, her eyes stinging with tears.

Connor was supposed to be coming here to pick her up for lunch. She was going to take tomorrow off so they could have a three-day weekend together. She prayed they'd both have those days together.

CONNOR PUSHED THE door open from the stairs. The reception area on this floor was empty, too. What the hell was going on?

"Stop."

A very young police officer beckoned to him from one of the office doors across the hall from Sloane's. He grabbed Connor's arm and tugged him into the room. "How did you get up here?"

"I came up the stairs. I'm here to pick up my girlfriend for lunch."

"My partner and I cleared the building. A man is holding two women hostage in the office across the hall."

Jesus! It had to be Sloane and Bernie.

Adrenaline hit his system like a punch and his heart rate sky-rocketed.

"I'm waiting for a hostage negotiation unit to arrive." Even as the young patrol officer spoke, the sound of booted feet carried down the hall, and he stepped to the door and beckoned to the group. All six men crowded into the small office.

As Connor listened to the young cop report how the whole thing had gone down, he wanted to punch something. They hadn't followed procedure and cuffed Reed Alexander because his boss asked for their discretion.

They'd put two women's lives at risk, and everyone else's, be-cause they hadn't handcuffed the son of a bitch. He wanted to punch that young cop, but instead he stood against the wall and tried to let the anger eating at him drain away.

One of the cops approached him. "Who are you, and why are you here?" Short and stocky, with gray hair and a flinty expression, he checked Connor out with the suspicious look of a veteran cop. He'd have to be if he was in charge of this unit. Connor glanced at the tag on his tactical vest. The patch said Sgt. Henry.

"I'm Chief Petty Officer Connor Evans. Sloane is my girl-friend. Bernie is her legal secretary and jack-of-all-trades in the office. And the man who's in there with them is Sloane's ex. Reed Alexander. They were engaged for two years, but it ended about eighteen months ago." He laid out the entire tangled situation for the cops, including Reed's aggressive behavior toward Sloane. "I can draw you a map of the layout of the Bernie's exterior office and Sloane's if you'd like."

"Do it. Get this man some paper. And get me some kind of communications going with this guy."

Connor spent five minutes drawing a map of both rooms, then handed it off to one of the men in the unit.

He'd been on rescue ops like this. SEALs didn't normally talk people down, because they were in areas where the tangos were killers and didn't really respond to a phone call. Reed Alexander wasn't a killer, but he was a bully. And he was desperate.

And he was holding Sloane, the woman he'd dreamed about for seven weeks. Couldn't get enough of when they were together. Was already building a life around. He was in love with her. Had been since that first night, that first kiss.

The cops were grouped around the drawings, still talking strategy, while another was focused on getting some kind of communications set up between them and Alexander. The office phone was off the hook and Alexander wasn't picking up his own phone.

Connor walked out of the room and across the hall to Bernie's office. He heard the shouts behind him, but just kept walking. Other than the damage to the doorframe and lock, the place appeared normal. He avoided looking at the pictures on the shelves behind Bernie's desk. Was her husband aware of what was happening? Possibly not. He couldn't allow himself to get emotional, though he'd become fond of Bernie.

He stood to one side of the door while he dialed Sloane's number and heard the ring inside her office.

Reed's voice came across the line, angry and belligerent. "Sloane can't come to the phone right now."

"I'm calling to talk to you, Reed. I'm standing just outside Sloane's office. Why don't you come out here so we can talk? You have the gun, and I'm not armed."

"No thanks. I'm safer in here with your *girlfriend*." He gave the word extra emphasis.

Through the crack in the door, Connor heard the feedback of his voice as he answered him. "You need to know that across the hall seven police officers in full tactical gear are waiting for the opportunity to bust in there and take you down.

"They're a hostage crisis team like SWAT. They'll try calling and talking to you, like I'm doing. Because you have a gun, they'll consider you a threat. And because you've taken Bernie and Sloane hostage, they'll assume you're a threat to them as well.

"They probably have the building surrounded by now, and they'll have snipers on the roofs of the buildings around us. So if you move close to any of the windows, they'll take you out."

He paused to let that sink in and let Reed stew on it for a moment. He heard the hitch in Reed's breathing as he realized the danger of his situation.

"I know you had to have some kind of emotional bond with Sloane when you were together. There isn't a man on the planet who couldn't develop feelings for her after spending five minutes together. She just draws you in and makes it impossible for you to keep your distance.

"I don't know what happened that turned your feelings for her in another direction, but she and Bernie don't deserve to have their lives put at risk. Let them come out."

Alexander remained silent for a moment. "I was never good enough for her. I knew it from the start."

Relief brought a momentary easing of tension to Connor's shoulders. This gave him a way to build a rapport with the man. "I'm not good enough for her either, but I'm trying to convince her I am."

He waited for Reed to speak, and when he didn't, he pushed on.

"Leave the gun on Sloane's desk and come out with them. You may have taken a wrong turn, but that doesn't mean your life has to be over. I took a wrong turn when my daughter died. I froze everyone out because I couldn't deal with the pain or the grief, and I lost my wife because of it.

"Sloane is my second chance. She means everything to me." He crushed down the emotions that threatened to rise.

"You can have a second chance, too, but you have to be alive to live it. Leave the gun on the desk and come out with Sloane and Bernie. Surrender, pay your dues, and then rebuild. Nothing has to end here. You can make it right."

REED HAD GONE still for several moments while silence hung between him and Connor. The gun hung slack in his hand. When he placed it on the desk beside the phone, Bernie's fingers tightened on her arm.

Tears streamed down Sloane's face, and she turned her face against Bernie's shoulder. The open emotion she heard in Connor's voice were a joy and a comfort, but the awful possibilities that hung over them all made it difficult to take it in.

She wanted out of this room so badly it took all her control not to leap to her feet and run for the door. But it would destroy everything Connor was trying to do.

There was defeat in Reed's expression when he looked up. "Sloane, you and Bernie need to get out of here." He leaned forward to rest his hands on his thighs, as though all his strength had drained out of him.

The two of them rose as one, still clinging to each other. Bernie's whole body shook. Sloane's legs felt just as shaky and uncooperative.

She kept her eye on Reed as they moved toward the door, fearful he'd change his mind and pick up the gun again. Bernie didn't waste any time dragging the table out of the way.

"Sloane."

She stiffened and turned to look at Reed, searching for the gun. It still lay on the desk.

"I'm sorry for everything. For it all. Everything that happened was all my doing. Everything I said when I ended it... I'm sorry."

She nodded. Maybe later it would matter to her, but right now all she wanted was to get away from him.

Connor waited just outside the door. He grabbed them both and held them for a second, then pushed them toward the door. "Go. I'll be right behind you."

Bernie ran for the door. Sloane held on. She wasn't going anywhere without him.

Connor's attention stayed on Reed. "Put your hands on your head and come with us. Surrender. It will go better for you if you do it voluntarily."

"Go be with Bernie." Connor's eyes brushed over her for a second. "I'll come out in a minute."

Sloane suddenly had a quick thought that Reed might commit suicide. He looked that defeated.

"Don't do anything you'll regret, Reed. We have a saying in the SEALs, 'the only easy day was yesterday.' Just take it a day at a time. You can do this."

Reed closed his eyes. "It's a relief to have lost it all. I can finally stop juggling a hundred balls at once, stealing, cheating." Tears streamed down his face. He put his hands on his head.

"I need to frisk you, Reed. They'll want to know you're truly unarmed."

He nodded.

Connor's arms tightened around Sloane briefly. "It'll be all right," he murmured against her ear. She released him.

He searched Reed just as a policeman would, running his hands over his limbs and body. From the way he did it, it wasn't his first time.

They walked next to Reed until they reached the door. Several guns were pointed at the doorway. Sloane gripped Connor's waist tighter, her heart in her throat.

"I've searched him," Connor said. "He's not armed, and he wants to surrender."

Connor tugged her out the door and moved aside, out into the reception area, away from the action as at least three men shouted for Reed to lie facedown on the floor. He quickly complied.

Sloane burrowed against Connor as tightly as she could. His arms were tight around her, his hand smoothing her hair over and over. The relief was almost numbing.

Once Reed was handcuffed, they hustled him out and down the stairs. One of the policemen broke away from others still milling about and approached them. His jaw worked, and he looked as though he'd like to take a swing at Connor. "I ought to arrest you for interfering with police business."

"I really hope you don't, sir. I only have a week left of leave, and I'd rather spend it with Sloane than in a jail cell. I'm about two months away from retirement from the Navy, and it might screw things up with my discharge, too."

The officer chewed on that a moment. "What the hell do you do for the Navy, Chief?" he asked.

"I'm a SEAL, sir."

"Well, hell." He shook his head and stomped off.

Connor looked down at her. "Do you think he'll come back and slap cuffs on me?"

"If he does, you have your lawyer right here."

He cupped her face in his hands, and his tender look had her eyes stinging. "I love you, Sloane."

Tears streamed down her face again. "I love you, too."

He brushed at the tears with his thumbs. "I want to build a family with you. I never thought I'd say that again. After Livy... But I'm saying it."

"Oh, Connor." She stretched up to kiss him. "It might be sooner than you're prepared for."

He tilted his head, looking confused. "What do you mean?"

She pulled the pregnancy test out of her bra and handed it to him.

He stared at the plus sign for several moments, then flashed a wry grin. "You said it would be a million-to-one shot." He laughed. "I've had a few of those during my SEAL career, but never one like this."

"What I said was true. My fallopian tubes were scarred by an infection when I was fourteen. My appendix burst, and I was in the hospital for a week. They told me I'd never be able to get pregnant without medical help."

He kissed her. "A miracle." His eyes were dark with emotion. "Our miracle."

Her chest felt as if her heart had swelled too big to fit properly. "Bernie says you have super-swimmers."

He laughed. "We haven't done anything slowly, have we?"

She shook her head. "No. I think I fell in love with you during our first date, our first kiss, Connor."

"You nearly brought me to my knees with that first kiss. If we keep this up, we may be in for a wild ride, Sloane." He rested his forehead against hers.

"You promised me an adventure."

He smiled. "Instead of just two weeks, we'll have a lifetime."

Which was more than fine with her.

MILITARY ROMANTIC SUSPENSE
BREAKING FREE (Book 1 of the SEAL Team Heartbreakers)
BREAKING THROUGH (Book 2 of the SEAL Team Heartbreakers)
BREAKING AWAY (Book 3 of the SEAL Team Heartbreakers)
BREAKING TIES (A SEAL Team Heartbreakers Novella)
BUILDING TIES (Book 4 of the SEAL Team Heartbreakers)
BREAKING BOUNDARIES (Book 5 of the SEAL Team Heartbreakers)
BREAKING OUT (BOOK 6 of the SEAL Team Heartbreakers)
BREAKING POINT (A SEAL Team Heartbreakers Novella)
BREAKING HEARTS (Book 7 of the SEAL Team Heartbreakers)

SEALS IN PARADISE SERIES
HOT SEALS, RUSTY NAIL

PARANORMAL ROMANCE
TIMELESS
DEEP WITHIN THE SHADOWS (Book 1 of the Superstition Series)
DEEP WITHIN THE STONE (Book 2 of the Superstition Series)
WHISPER IN MY EAR
HAVE WAND, WILL TRAVEL (Book 1)
HAVE WAND, WILL TRAVEL: ONCE BITTEN, TWICE SHY (Book 2)
HAVE WAND, WILL TRAVEL: ADVENTURES OF A WITCHY
WALLFLOWER (Book 3)

HISTORICAL ROMANCE
CAPTIVE HEARTS
HIGHLAND MOONLIGHT
TO CAPTURE A HIGHLANDER'S HEART: THE TRILOGY

The Highland Moonlight Spinoff Trilogy in parts
TO CAPTURE A HIGHLANDER'S HEART: THE BEGINNING
TO CAPTURE A HIGHLANDER'S HEART: THE COURTSHIP
TO CAPTURE A HIGHLANDER'S HEART: THE WEDDING NIGHT

SHORT STORIES
AN AUTOMATED DEATH: A STEAMPUNK SHORT STORY
CAUGHT IN THE ACT: A HUMOROUS SHORT STORY

CHILDREN'S BOOK
WILLY C. SPARKS, THE DRAGON WHO LOST HIS FIRE